A STRANGER WITH A BAG

# A STRANGER
# WITH A BAG

AND OTHER STORIES

SYLVIA TOWNSEND WARNER

*faber and faber*

This edition first published in 2011
by Faber and Faber Ltd
Bloomsbury House, 74–77 Great Russell Street
London WC1B 3DA

The right of Sylvia Townsend Warner to be identified as author of this work
has been asserted in accordance with Section 77 of the
Copyright, Designs and Patents Act 1988

A CIP record for this book is available from the British Library

ISBN 978-0-571-28010-0

*To*
DAVID GARNETT

With the exception of *A Jump Ahead* and *Total Loss* all these stories were first published in 'The New Yorker' to whom my thanks are due.

# CONTENTS

# A STRANGER WITH
# A BAG

AFTER three years as a travelling salesman Clive Peters supposed he knew every detail of the East Anglian landscape he covered, whether he went southward to Bungay and Beccles or inland through the Cambridgeshire fens. The firm that employed him was old-fashioned and without enterprise; he only went out two days a week, working the rest of the time in the office as a clerk. The landscape through which he travelled, going by local trains—for the previous salesman had met his death in a car accident, for which Mr. Ingham, a paternal employer, had never ceased to blame himself—from one market town to another, was not the sort of landscape in which details escape one's attention. If a new milking shed were built or an old barn pulled down or a tree uprooted by the gales that blew in from the North Sea Clive would have noticed it and marked it down in his memory as an event and something to speculate about. But now, glancing out of the train window, he saw a house that had never been there before. Square and sombre and planted massively behind a screen of overgrown laurels and tossing ilexes, it looked as though the time of the year had put it there, a corroboration of the dark waterlogged November fields and the dull sky.

But really it was just that he had never happened to notice it before. It was quite an old house; it must have been there for years. It stood about half a mile from the track—too far to see it as more than a picture. He had an

instant conviction that it was uninhabited, which on examination he traced to the fact that though this was a
Monday there was no washing out. It was a house in
which there would be no place for a spin dryer. Everything
would be done in the old way: the washing pegged to a
line, the pork meat for pies and galantines chopped with a
sharp knife on a wooden board, the carpets swept with tea
leaves. The spell had fallen on him so completely that
simultaneously he knew the house to be uninhabited and
knew all about its former inhabitants: chapelgoers; upright, hard-working, close-fisted, bleakly suspicious of all
customs but their own, yet secreting a kind of sturdy cosi-
ness, bred of duty and self-satisfaction. While they lived
there, the core of the house was safety and prosperity.
Now they were gone, and the house remained for his
possession—a solemn plaything.

The house slid out of sight but remained solidly in his
mind. He saw himself approaching it, the figure in the
foreground. Presently he was near enough to hear the
swish of the ilexes, the laurels' dry rattle. In the garden,
hoary gooseberry bushes were laced with strings of last
summer's bindweed; trailing brambles caught at his feet
but did not delay him. The house was certainly empty.
Sure enough, on its weather side a back door had rotted
from its hinges. He walked in, meeting the raw smell of a
cold hearth, a smell mixed of soot and rusty iron. He went
up the stairs and wandered from room to room. In one of
them a discolouring illuminated text flapped on the wall,
stirred by the wind blowing down the chimney. 'Be Ye
Also Ready.' In a garland of wheat and poppies.

He was too deeply absorbed to notice the train slowing
down. Now it stopped. The station was called Yetton

Halt; he had never known the train to stop there before. He heard a voice say 'Here you are, Bill' and a heavy parcel thrown down on the platform. Before he knew what he was doing he got out, carrying his bag of samples. Before he could think better of it the train was moving on. Bill was walking away with the parcel; there was no one else about. Clive thought, If I am killed, there will be no one to give evidence that I left the train at Yetton Halt. The thought pleased him. In his regular days between work and home, there was no room for even a possible anonymity. Outside the station a road branched east and west, and he turned eastward.

Though he was uncertain how far away the house might be he judged it could not lie more than three or four miles back. Standing alone and within sight of the railway it should be easy to find; if he guided himself by the railway he must hit it, sooner or later. For a mile or so the road kept level with the railway, then it veered suddenly and went under the track by a tunnel. It would be fatal to get on the wrong side of the track, so he retraced his steps to where he had noticed a lane which branched off in the direction he wanted. The lane ran zigzagging between tall hedges; he soon lost his sense of orientation, and whenever he came to a left-hand gate and looked hopefully over it, some obstacle, a further hedge or a stand of tall winter kale, interposed itself between him and any chance sight of the railway telegraph poles. But he kept on, and felt a kind of obstinate enjoyment. He was splashed with mud, his arms ached from the weight of the bag, it was nearly half past two and he had left his parcel of sandwiches in the train, he was behaving like a madman and would have to account for it; but it was a break, and worth it.

He was still obstinately enjoying himself when he heard an engine whistle. With a burst of joy that denounced his previous enjoyment, he scrambled through the hedge and began to run across country. He ran on and on, scattering a herd of bullocks, setting up a flock of curlews feeding in a marshy meadow. He swung himself over a gate into a rickyard where blown chaff streamed across his vision like a sallow snowstorm. He stooped under a strand of barbed wire, stood up, dizzied with breathlessness, and saw the row of telegraph poles and the railway track. The train had vanished, but the smell of coal smoke remained.

So now he had only to find the house. He walked on soberly, in line with the railway track, and presently, as in a dream, the house reappeared, and was instantly recognizable, though, as in a dream, it looked quite different. Seen from ground level it lacked the compactness and drama of its first presentation and had an upstart, ungainly appearance, its chimneys too tall, its roof too sharply pitched and furbelowed by ornate bargeboards. It was smaller, too, than he had supposed.

It was not so easy of access, either. The ilexes and laurels were fenced in by a railing of tall iron spikes and he had to walk to the farther side before he found the gate, which was approached by a track across a muddy pasture— branching off, no doubt, from some farm lane, for he could hear the shouting voice of a man driving cows. The gate was of iron, like the fencing, and with the same air of having been brought from a town. Beyond the gate a path, running between a laurel hedge and a shaggy lawn on which there were some rabbit hutches, led to the front door and on round the corner of the house. Clive followed it, because in his imagined house the door rotted from its hinges had been a back door. The compulsion of the imagined house was stronger than the disenchantment of what he saw; and it still seemed to him that if he went on he would find the door rotted from its hinges, and make his way into that other house and go upstairs and read the text bordered with wheat and poppies. Meanwhile the rational part of him continued to make the rational assertion that, having come so far, it would be poor-spirited to give up his intention just because the house turned out to be uninviting and rather pretentious with its lowering barge-boards and oversized sash windows. Looking with sidelong distaste at one of these windows he saw a boy, whose pale face was pressed to the glass, whose eyes were fixed on him. A moment later the vision disappeared, for the boy's breath had been released and misted over the pane. A skinny hand wiped the mist away and the face looked out once more, with the stare of a full moon emerging from a cloud.

As though the staring gaze had shown it to him, Clive saw what the boy was looking at. A stranger, carrying a bag. Of course, that was the answer. He smiled at the boy, who did not return his smile, walked back to the front door, mounted its pretentious steps and pulled the bell handle. He heard no footsteps, but presently the door opened and the boy stood on the threshold. He looked to be about ten years old, very near the age of Clive's own son, but small for his age.

'Anyone in, Sonny?'

'Be,' said the boy, who had a cold in his head.

'I wonder if I can interest you in these samples of floor and furniture polish.' Clive opened the bag. 'All made locally, with real beeswax. You don't find many polishes nowadays with the real beeswax. Perhaps if I leave this card, you could tell your mother.'

'I habn't got a bother now. She went away last Tuesday, with Jib Bason. I saw theb go off together, on his botor bike. And Dad says he won't hab her back, not if she came on her bended knees.'

Shaking off the impression that there must be something superlatively appealing about a mended knee, Clive said, 'Oh dear!' and then, 'I'm sure I'm sorry.'

'So ab I. I liked Jib. He bade me laugh.'

Clive looked at the skinny, unappetizing child, framed against the recession of that long, dark passage and the stairway ascending under the bleak glare of another of those oversized windows, and thought that Jim Mason must have talents for the impossible. One could imagine a woman's laugh flaring out in such a house; but not the laughter of a child. And there was nothing he could do about it. And pity was unavailing.

'You mustn't stand here, Sonny. You'll make that cold of yours worse. And I must be going.'

He stooped and fastened the bag. A stranger with a bag. Well, at least he had supplied a brief diversion, an incident in a winter afternoon.

'Cub in,' said the boy.

'Why, Sonny, that's very nice of you. I wish I could. But I'm on my rounds, you see. And I've got a long way to go yet.'

'Cub in,' the boy repeated.

'And what would your dad say? I don't suppose he'd approve of you asking strangers into the house.'

'*Cub in.*' The boy's voice, which his cold rendered totally expressionless, rose to a peremptory shriek.

'Cub in, cub in, cub in!' His hands fastened on Clive's wrist like pincers, like red-hot pincers, for they were burning with fever.

'Well, for two minutes, then. Just to settle you back by the fire and see that you're comfortable.'

The boy flitted down the passage before him and opened a door into a high-ceilinged room. It was cold and cavernous and the glow of a small electric heater darkened it rather than warmed it.

'Is this where you've been sitting all this afternoon?'

The boy was shaking up a cushion and did not reply.

'Dull work, having to nurse a cold, isn't it? Still, better indoors than out on a day like this. What rain we've been having! And gales, too.'

A train was passing; the reverberation in the chimney seemed to decant it into the room. But he's too old for trains now, thought Clive.

'Though I don't suppose gales mean much to you in a house like this. It looks uncommonly solid. Built to last.'

The boy was still fidgeting with the armchair. Having beaten up its cushions, he was now diving into the cranny between the back and the seat. Clive walked about the room, trying to make conversation.

'Are those your rabbits, in the hutches near the gate?'

'They were.' After so long a silence it was almost disconcerting to be answered. 'But now we hab eaten theb. We ate old Roger yesterday.'

The statement was so flat that it was not even unfeeling.

'When I was your age, I had a tame rat. I used to take it to school with me, in my pocket, and one day—I say, Sonny, what's that? Take care you don't cut yourself.'

The boy had somehow produced a carving knife and was fingering the blade.

'And that's not the way to handle it, running your finger across its edge. You must use your finger and thumb if you want to feel how sharp it is. I'll show you.' He took the knife and demonstrated. 'Sharp as a razor. Let me tell you, you were very lucky not to give yourself a nasty cut. Well, here you are. Be more careful next time.'

The boy put his hands behind his back and shook his head vehemently. 'No! It's for you.'

'But, Sonny, I don't want a carving knife.'

'It's for you.'

Half mad with loneliness, thought Clive. His mother's gone off with a man, his rabbits are eaten, he's got nothing to care for; then I come along, a romantic stranger.

'I want you to burder Dad.'

'What!'

'I want you to burder Dad.'

'Is that what you asked me in for?' said Clive, after a pause.

The boy nodded. A delicate pink colour had come into his cheeks; his eyes glittered.

Clive laid the knife on the table and sat down in the armchair. It was a more fatherly attitude—and his knees were shaking. 'Now, look here, Sonny. This sort of thing won't do. I suppose you've been watching the tellie.'

'We habn't got a tellie. Dad wouldn't get one. We neber hab anything like other people do. Burder hib, burder hib! It's all he's good for.'

'Blow your nose,' said Clive. 'What, lost your handker chief? Have mine, then. Now, listen to me. I'm not going to murder your dad. Neither are you. Murder's a fool's game—not to mention a crime. Do you ever feel afraid?'

The boy glanced at the black mouth of the chimney, then out of the window at the tossing ilexes.

'I can tell you this. Whatever you may feel afraid of, a murderer feels ten times more afraid, a million times more afraid. And because he's a murderer, he's afraid of everything, everyone he meets, every knock at the door, every noise——'

The noise was quite perceptible, and was the noise of a bicycle being wheeled along the path. 'There's Dad,' said the boy.

Clive leaped up. The bicycle was being wheeled past the window; presumably there was a shed at the back of the house. There was still time for him to get away. At the same moment, the boy switched on the light. It lit up the small, dejected figure of a man with a pointed beard. He turned and saw Clive standing by the window. His look of oppression deepened. He attempted to prop the bicycle against a bush. At each attempt, the bush gave way and the bicycle subsided. Finally he left it lying, and turned towards the front door. While the door was opened and carefully closed again, and a swishing mackintosh shaken and hung on a peg, and a tread that would have better matched a larger man came along the passage, Clive avoided looking at the boy.

'Hullo, Tony! I see you've got a visitor.'

Clive began to explain, reopening the bag and drawing out a couple of tins to substantiate his words. The sound of his voice embarrassed him—it was so full and ringing, so grossly unlike the flat, dejected tones that replied.

'Hmm. Yes, I see. Very kind of you, I'm sure. But I'm afraid I don't want any polish just now.'

'No, no! Of course not. I quite understand.'

The words were no sooner spoken than Clive realized their appalling appropriateness. He hurried on. 'And I'm sure it's a reward in itself to be asked in so kindly by Sonny here.'

Mentioning the boy, he dared to glance towards him, and saw the knife still lying on the table. 'To tell the truth, I've always been rather interested by this house. I often notice it from the train. Quite a period piece, isn't it? Puts one in mind of Dickens—Pickwick, and What-d'you-call-it Hall, and that house in the marshes where the old lady lived.'

'Yes. They don't build such houses nowadays. It's got the date over the door—I don't know if you observed it. 1887. Same date as Queen Victoria's Jubilee. You could call it historic.'

'Neber had an alteration since,' interposed the boy, as though repeating something known by rote.

'Yes, it has, Tony. You know it has. It's got the electricity. And I've a good mind to take it out again—nothing but trouble from first to last. I don't know why anyone should complain of a house like this. It's a splendid house; everything of the best, and built by an Indian colonel to retire to. Got its own water supply, and a patent pump to raise it, and a game larder, and any number of cupboards, and a marble pedestal basin in the downstairs lavatory. You'd think anyone would be happy to live in such a house. So they would be, if they feared God and knew what was best for them.'

'The rats do! They know what's best for theb. That's

why Bother slept with be—to keep the rats off. But now I'b going to tabe theb. I'b going to hab billions and billions of tabe rats. This man said he had a tabe rat and he took it to school with hib in his pocket.'

The chin beard, as though it had a life of its own quite independent of the meagre flesh it was fastened in, suddenly bristled.

'So it's you that have been putting ideas into the boy's head, is it? That's what you've been coming here for, whenever my back was turned? I knew it, I knew it! But I tell you, I've had too much of that sort of thing. First there's Jim Mason going off with my wife, now it's you, sneaking in after my boy. And what's that knife meant for, lying there on the table? There you were in the dark, waiting to get me as soon as I came into the room. You and your polishes! You and your soft sawder about books you've never read in your life. No need to read nowadays, you can see it all on the tellie. Yes, and pick up those clever ideas about carving knives. But two can play at that game!'

He snatched the knife, and attacked. Clive caught up a chair to defend himself.

'I'll get you, I'll get you!'

Lungeing at Clive, he became entangled in the legs of the chair and fell, pulling the chair down with him. The knife was jolted from his grasp; he lay sprawled face downward, gasping for breath. A small trail of blood appeared on the carpet.

The boy darted forward, light as a ferret. 'He's bleeding! He's dying!'

'He's hit his nose against the chair,' Clive said. 'And presently, I suppose, *he'll* be wanting a handkerchief, too. Well, I can't oblige him, that's all. Here, take that knife and for God's sake put it back where it belongs. I'm sick of the pair of you.' It seemed to him that he had invaded a very disagreeable family.

After a minute the man sat up. He was weeping, and mopped his eyes and his nose alternately. 'I can't go on, I just can't go on,' he lamented. 'God knows I've always done my best—and look what happens to me. I love my wife, I don't look at another woman, I take her out of Woolworth's and put her in this splendid house and make a lady of her, I slave to keep the roof over our heads—and she goes off to live in a bungalow with a motor mechanic! I do everything I can for the boy, I keep a smiling face for his sake, I get up in the middle of the night to boil milk for him—and he hates me! And today, when I go to see my lawyer, first he keeps me waiting for nearly an hour, and then he tells me I can't ask for damages, not for the wife of my bosom, because it's common knowledge how un-kindly I treated her. Unkindly! What about the way she's treated me? And there you stand, grinning. Grin on, grin by all means! Your time hasn't come yet.'

'I wouldn't dream of laughing at you,' Clive said. 'I'm sure I'm very sorry for you.' But he knew that he had smiled. For the man's nose, rapidly swelling, made him talk just as the boy did, and the words 'get up in the biddle of the night to boil bilk' had been too much for him.

The boy had opened a book and feigned to be absorbed in it. His hate no longer warmed him; he sat hunched up and shivering—a sickly child, in terror of rats and dark corners and swaying trees. But suffering and depravity had put their aristocratic stamp on his pallid face; there could be no doubt which of these two would be master.

Dad was now on his feet, rubbing his shins and groaning.

'You don't happen to have such a thing as a bottle of liniment in that bag, I suppose?'

'I'm afraid not.'

'I might have known it!' He spoke as though this were the culmination of his misfortunes and injuries.

'And I really must be getting on,' Clive said. 'Good night. Don't trouble to show me out. I know the way.'

He saw the beard begin to bristle again, and the fury of suspicion mounting. The boy must have seen it too, though he continued to read. A smile crossed his face as though something in the book had amused him.

'Tony!' the man said. 'Where are your manners? Get up and say good night.'

The boy rose, and bowed with formality. 'Good night.'

\*

'Just in time,' said Clive, slamming the door behind him and running down the path. 'Whew! Just in time.' At the same moment, the laurel hedge caught him in a dragonish embrace and remembering the rabbit hutches he went on more cautiously. It was the ambiguous interval of winter nightfall when one seems to be wading through darkness as through knee-high water while there is still light overhead. But soon it would be unequivocally dark and though he was out of that nightmare house he had still to find his way home. Ahead of him was the lane where he had heard the man shouting at cows. It seemed likely that this was a continuation of the lane he had followed so patiently and which would have brought him here if he had not left it at the call of the engine whistle. His best hope would be to turn to the right and follow its windings till it joined the road he had taken from Yetton Halt. He did so, and had walked for what seemed quite a long way when a picture came into his mind's eye of himself sitting at Yetton Halt watching trains that didn't stop there go by. But how to get home wasn't his only trouble. He must also decide on a story that would somehow account for him being so muddy and so belated, a story that would satisfy Ella tonight and Mr. Ingham tomorrow—for Ella being Mrs. Ingham's niece he could not expect the story to remain under his own roof. 'I tripped and wrenched my ankle.' But if he had tripped anywhere on the path of duty there would have been a telephone within reach. 'I got into the wrong train at the junction.' But the train would not have carried him into a ploughed field and muddied him to the knees. 'I heard there was a family who had just moved into an old manor house with masses of oak panelling.' But Mr. Ingham had little sympathy for enterprise, and would have even less for an enterprise that had not resulted in as much as an order for a three-shilling tin of Busy Bees Household Wax —their cheapest line. So what was he to say? And which way should he turn in order to say it? As he stood hesitating and hearing the wind mutter along the hedge, he saw a shaft of light and heard the approach of what must be a very old and slow car. The slower the better. He might thumb a lift. The car, bouncing and rattling, seemed to be close at hand, but its light travelled onwards. There must be a crossroads. If it were enough of a crossroads, it would have a signpost. He hurried on.

There was a signpost, but he had to swarm up it before he could read by the flicker of his cigarette lighter that to his left was Branham, five miles, and to his right Yetton St. Gabriel, two miles. Branham had it. He knew Branham, it was a place on his rounds. He lit a cigarette, knocked the worst of the mud off his shoes and set off again, this time on a good hard-surfaced road that rang reassuringly under his tread. Now all he had to think of was his story. Why not, after all, include a measure of the interesting truth, leading up to it by that hearsay manor house? He was on his way to the manor house, which was much farther off than it had been reported to be, when he noticed a solitary house which stood a little back from the road and had a sort of moat round it. The strange thing was that even before he drew level with it, he felt as though the house had a call for him. If it had not been for one lighted-up window, he would have supposed it was empty and deserted. Then, glancing through the lighted window, he saw a man with a knife in his hand chasing a little boy round a table. Not wasting a moment, he jumped the moat, ran to the window and banged on it, shouting, 'You leave that child alone!' The man threw open the window and leaned out, saying, 'Mind your own business!' 'Just what I mean to do,' retorted Clive, and sprang in over the window sill. At this point Mr. Ingham's voice interposed itself, exclaiming, 'It's a case for the Prevention of Cruelty Society, Peters, if not for the police. We'll report this right away,' while Mrs. Ingham cried, 'You tell me where he lives, Clive, and I'll teach him something about carving knives, that I will!' So no sooner was Clive in the room than the man's whole demeanour changed; dropping the knife he came up to Clive and wrung his hand, saying, 'God must have sent you, God must have sent you! What mightn't I have done otherwise?' And then, bit by bit, it all came out: how the man's wife had left him that same morning, how when he got back from market he had found her gone and a letter saying she wanted an easier life with a younger man, how he had found the child cold and hungry and crying for his mammy, and how, in his desperation, he had decided to put an end to himself—but first he must take the child with him. Clive, feeling that he had indeed been called, realized that there was nothing for it but to give up all idea of the manor house and stay with the frantic husband till he calmed down again. ('Quite right, Peters, quite right.') So he quickly kindled up a nice wood fire, and there they sat, going into it all, till it was time to turn on the news. This helped to clear the air, and after a little more chat Clive rose to depart, seeing that his work was done. 'I don't suppose we'll ever meet again,' were the man's last words. 'But I'll remember you in my prayers for the rest of my life.' Deeply religious, which made the wife's action an even crueller blow, he was more to be pitied than blamed.

*More to be Pitied than Blamed. Pom! More to be Pitied than Blamed. Pom!* Marching to the rhythm of the words, carried on towards Branham by their asseveration, Clive felt that he had got both truth and fiction safely under his control. The story was certainly a case of making a silk purse out of a sow's ear, but he had managed it; the purse was constructed, and ought to satisfy everybody. All that remained was to put the true afternoon firmly out of his mind and rehearse the fictional one till he was word-perfect in it. Manor house to house, not forgetting the premonition, then the lighted-up window, then the man with the carving knife and the terrified child dodging him round the table, then the banging on the window and the window thrown up and his retort (another touch not to forget) and his entry. . . . Suddenly and appallingly, Ella's voice broke in. 'But what about the poor little boy, Clive? Didn't you do anything for him? Didn't either of you men think of giving him his supper? You said he was hungry.' The sow's ear bristled out of the purse, the real child started up before him, dancing like a ferret at the sight of his father's blood. No wonder he had shirked facing the issue of the fictional child. He, too, was the father of a son.

# JOHNNIE BREWER

It was nine years since Johnnie Brewer last saw his grand-mother and his great-aunt Miranda. Then he was a boy, and a visitor from Australia. Now he was a young man, and a returning exile. They had remained two old ladies, two typical old English ladies, living in a country house whose lawn had daisies on it. The lawn he looked down on from the spare room window was smaller than he remembered; but he was larger, which accounted for this. There was the lawn roller, just where it used to be, its handle sunk in the laurel bush. Probably the same toad lived behind it. Toads live to a great age. Spring after spring they amble out into the same patch of sunlight and snap at this year's flies on the same warm wall. Year after year (while he in the antipodes had been substantiating his nostalgia for a country he had barely seen, and poring over maps and guide books and poetry and manuals on British birds and British wild flowers, and plastering his bedroom walls with photographs from National Trust calendars) the two old dames below had been leading their rich English lives, going out to pick the first snowdrops, watching their pears ripen, seeing the first swallows arrive and the last swallows depart.

He bounded downstairs for tea and burst in on them as they sat with a wood fire burning and yet the window open on the garden, and the smooth fresh faces of old family portraits looking over their heads, and the silver teapot and the green-and-white tea set on the damask cloth. The thought of their accumulated good fortune overwhelmed him, and he exclaimed, 'Oh, you lucky old darlings, you've been here all the time!'

'Dear Johnnie! I hope you won't see many changes,' said his great-aunt.

His grandmother said, 'At any rate, it's the same chocolate cake. We've still got old Woodie, you know.'

'I know you have. I've been hugging her in the kitchen, behind your backs.'

Their light English laughter was like something out of a musical-box.

'You mustn't make us jealous,' said his grandmother. 'I hope you had a pleasant drive here.'

'It was a wonderful drive. I lost my way.'

'Oh, dear!'

'And I got into the most amazing valley, with pear trees in bloom all the way along it. Very narrow, very winding, with steep sides—and pear trees everywhere. Would they be wild, do you think? Or old orchards? And a stream with an old humped stone bridge. And a ruin.'

'Goodness! I wonder where this was.'

'He must have got into the old Monmouth road.'

'I don't remember any ruins there. More likely the road to Pentrice. We used to go that way to the Watsons'.'

'We never went over a bridge.'

They argued with animation, and he sat remembering the green-and-white hillsides he would remember all his life, the stream rattling over the stones, the birds singing. He had halted the car and got out and drunk the cold stream-water from his cupped hands, saying to himself, 'Now it will always fetch me back.' And the chill, the delicate pure chill of the watery valley, had made him quiver with ecstasy.

The car was a hired one. His father had said, 'Now mind. The legacy's your own; you can do what you like with it. But two things you are not to do. You are not to buy any English investments, and you are not to buy a car.' He could not prohibit marrying an English wife, since he had done so himself.

Johnnie worked his passage as a deck steward, made a good haul of tips and arrived at Tilbury Docks when April was there. Climbing onto a bus, he went to Greenwich, where he saw Greenwich Hospital and Greenwich Observatory and sat in Greenwich Park looking at the curve of the river. Then, as it was still early in the day, he went on to St. Paul's.

By the end of a week, Johnnie was a Londoner. By the end of the following week, he was so much a Londoner that he felt he must spend a weekend in the country. He hired a car and drove into Oxfordshire. There, in a mild rain, he sat on a grass bank and looked at primroses. He also ate bread and cheese at an inn with a faded Charles I on its swinging sign, where a commercial traveller came in, saying he had heard the first cuckoo; and attended evensong—with more primroses—in a village church. England had forty-one counties. He would visit them all. Having done this, he would be in a better position to decide where he would ultimately live. England also contained castles, cathedrals, an unknown number of the oldest yew trees in England, Devil's Dykes, Devil's Cheese Rings, Stonehenge and his grandmother. In his pocket was a letter from his mother saying, 'Whatever else you do, don't forget to go and see Grannie. But ask her beforehand. Her address, in case you've forgotten it. . .' He hadn't forgotten it. Bodkins, Dishpole St. Mary's, Herefordshire. That earlier visit had been in August. It rained a lot, but he went fishing, and played beggar-my-neighbour with Woodie in the warm spicy kitchen while his mother sat talking to Grandmother and Aunt Miranda. At the time, it all seemed rather tame, but now he would know how to appreciate it —a night or perhaps a couple of nights in a gentle English home where the streets would smell of lavender. It would be a change from sleeping in hotels, too; and afterwards he would drive on and explore Wales. He wrote suggesting himself, and was told in reply that any date that suited him would suit them, and that he was to stay as long as he liked.

'No, Hester, I've got it. He must have come by the road that turns off just after Dunnock's Cross. And that ruin must be the old Congregationalist chapel. Somebody or other told me that it had fallen down last winter; the roof gave way under the snow.'

'Did you have a lot of snow here, Grandmother?'

'Far too much. We were snowed up for over a week. We nearly went out of our minds trying to feed the birds. We soon ran out of bread, of course, but we chopped up all the apples and carrots and potatoes. Miranda said she'd toboggan down to the village. So she sat on the kitchen tea tray and Woodie and I gave her a good shove off. Have a cigarette?'

'No, thank you, Grandmother. I don't smoke.'

'But she ran into a tree and tore all the skin off her leg, and the tea tray went on without her. They found it in the churchyard, after the thaw. And that was the end of her girlish dreams, poor Miranda!'

'But didn't anyone come to your help?'

'In the end. But they had to dig the animals out first. Naturally.'

'The truth is,' said Aunt Miranda, 'it's damned silly for two old hags like Hester and me to go on living here. We ought to be in a home for decayed gentlewomen. Have a cigarette?'

'No, thank you, Aunt Miranda. I don't——'

'He doesn't smoke,' said his grandmother. 'You're getting deaf, Miranda. He said so not a minute ago.'

When Woodie came in to clear away, he glanced at his watch. It was earlier than he thought. He would take himself out for a walk—an English stroll.

His grandmother noticed the glance and said, 'What would you like to do between now and dinner, dear boy?'

'I'd rather like to—— Here, Woodie! I'll carry that tray.'

Out in the passage, Woodie said, 'Do you know what you ought to do, Master Johnnie? You ought to offer to take them for a drive.'

He had expected them to go upstairs and reappear in bonnets, but they unhitched some wraps from a stand in the hall and came out hatless, though pulling on gloves. He gave a hasty tidy to the back of the car and held open the rear door, ready to help them in. Miranda got nimbly into the front seat. 'Miranda's always sick in the back of a car,' his grandmother explained. Miranda smirked as though he had been told something to her credit.

He said they must direct him where to go, and once again they began to argue about roads. Now the argument involved a debate as to whether they could get to Hereford in time to do some shopping, and feeling the lovely spring evening slipping away while they bandied possibilities he asserted, 'I shall just drive.' Instantly they agreed.

As he drove down the village street houses, flagged paths, names on shop fronts assaulted him with their familiarity. He could have sworn that a white cat sitting on a gatepost had not moved from its position since some unidentified encounter nine years ago. He drove on. A name on a signpost, meaningless then but now dipped in the melancholy lustre of *A Shropshire Lad*, drew him into a succession of lanes. Beyond the hedges, the meadows, starred with kingcups and cuckoo-pint, were like jewels displayed in small compartments. Lambs were feeding in orchards, black-and-white farmhouses sent up tendrils of smoke against the sharp green of newly-leafed sycamores, steeples came twirling towards him as the lanes twisted, houses of Victorian gentility stood among conifers. After a while, the name out of *A Shropshire Lad* did not recur. Miranda and his grandmother kept up a succession of anecdotes about people of the locality, and he was intermittently conscious that they were trying to entertain him. As for the beauty of the evening, they seemed blind to it though they must have noticed where he was driving them, since when he pointed to a beechwood, an apparition of river, the lovely slope of a hillside, they promptly supplied its name. He could have wished they had not smoked so much, and so often set each other right over details—for really it could not matter to him whether a Captain Hughes had died in 1955 or 1957. But it was a wonderful drive, and a foretaste of what it would be like when he drove alone. He had given them pleasure, too. Miranda, turning to the back seat, had suddenly exclaimed, 'Hester! Isn't this fun?' And his grandmother had replied, 'Glorious! Scrumptious!' and then, more explicitly, 'I can't tell you, Johnnie, what a treat it is to have an unexpected outing like this.

33

We shall talk about it for months.' Her gratitude touched him, and he said, 'I hope I'm not driving too fast for you.' They assured him that driving fast was part of the fun; but the jolting in the back seat must have tired his grandmother, for she had to be helped out and supported up the path, clinging to his arm and saying he was a dear boy, her dear boy.

'So sweet of you to come all this way to see us!'

It was the tone in which one adulates a child. He felt he was being made over into the Johnnie of that first visit—and didn't like it.

'It wasn't far out of my way at all,' he said.

Miranda passed them and went upstairs whistling. When she came down, she was wearing earrings.

During dinner, his grandmother remarked, 'You wouldn't think that Miranda was five years older than me, would you?'

'I don't know that I ever think much about old age,' he replied. In case this did not fulfil all demands on tactfulness, he went on to ask how old Woodie was.

'You had better ask her yourself,' said his grandmother.

'All we know is that she's been lying about it for years,' added Miranda.

Johnnie laughed. There was something cronyish and releasing about his Aunt Miranda. Of the two, it was she he preferred. She was easier to talk to, asking him questions about himself; she did not weigh on his senses, as his grandmother did. Yet obviously his grandmother had the greater tenderness for him (as was natural), and he felt rather uncivil in preferring his great-aunt. To tell the truth, he did not like either of them as much as he had intended to. They were no duller than he remembered and considerably more

34

attentive. But they had not kept step with his increasing regard for them; they were not the two wonderful old English ladies, dwelling in the dignified past, who had lent their actuality to his vision of a country he would come back to from half a world away, and whom, only a meal ago, he had hailed with his 'You've been here all the time!' At best, they were two typically English old things, dwelling with childish excitement on that one phenomenal winter when they had tossed up for the last cigarette and, starving themselves, gone out in blizzards to feed birds. Yes, that was how they would figure in his memories: two gallant, bird-loving old English eccentrics, sitting below family portraits and eating small warm fragments of smoked haddock on squares of moist toast—for by now dinner had reached that English achievement, the savoury. He had met it already in a hotel, under the name of Canapé Ivanhoe.

He realized that he had fallen silent and that they both were looking at him. He began to ask questions about the family portraits, and Miranda offered to show him one in her bedroom which was almost certainly a Lawrence. But at that moment Woodie announced that coffee was served in the drawing room, and after coffee he found himself drawn down onto his grandmother's sofa to look at snapshots of his mother as a little girl, smiling the same gapped smile on beaches in Norfolk, moors in Scotland, and as an attendant on Britannia in a school play. Her second teeth must have been unusually slow in coming—his had been, too; it must be a family thing. He was not able to pursue this, for now his grandmother had opened another album, going back to the days of her own youth: his great-grandfather, winter-sporting; Miranda with dachshunds; his grandmother playing tennis on a grass court, smiling in a hammock, throwing a snowball. She seemed to be snow-balling behind smoked glass, for she had turned the pages backwards, and the snapshots were increasingly yellowed and shadowy.

'Which winter was that?' asked Miranda, who had come to look over their shoulders. His grandmother turned on to another page, and would have flipped it over but Miranda's hand came down on it. 'And do you know who these are?' It was a professional photograph and its glossy efficiency made it look far more out-dated than the snap-shots. It showed two little girls. One sat bolt upright, her hands tightly folded on her lap, her long plaits falling over her shoulders; the other, a younger child, had been arranged by the photographer to nestle against her. Both glared re-sentfully at the camera. 'That's Hester.' Miranda's finger stabbed at the child with the plaits. 'The other one's me. And would you believe it—I was three years younger than your grandmother then.'

His grandmother said, 'That's enough!' and shut the album with a bang. The movement tilted her up against him; she was so close that her explosion of anger seemed to spatter him like a hot wave. Suddenly feeling affronted, he got to his feet and said without forethought of what he was saying, 'Do you mind if I go to bed?'

Together, they accompanied him to his room, talking about the long day's driving, the effects of country air. They made sure there was a hot-water bottle in his bed, biscuits on the bedside table; they offered him hot milk, they explained that there were extra blankets in the bot-tom drawer of the bureau, and that the coffin-shaped stain on the ceiling was where the snow had seeped through during the thaw. When they had gone, he threw open the casement window and leaned out, listening for a nightingale. There was an old English saying about nightingales: 'East of the Severn, south of the Trent.' He was west of the Severn, so it was vain to listen for a nightingale, but the saying itself was a kind of music. He knew it, and could apply it; and that morning he had crossed the Severn at Gloucester, where the east window in the cathedral, a great wall of glass, is the largest in England, and a murdered English King lies buried. By this time tomorrow night he would be in Wales, where road gradients are one in four and the last wolf was killed. For he would not change his mind and stay another night at Bodkins. It had been built in 1753, and they were his English relatives, and he would certainly come back another time. But he needed to go away before he could reconcile himself to them being so unlike his expectations—smoking so many cigarettes, eating so greedily and taunting each other with age and infirmity.

Down in the village a church clock chimed out the hour, and from far away in the calm night another church clock repeated it at a slower pace. He undressed and got into bed, catching his breath at the fineness of the linen sheets.

It seemed to him that he had scarcely fallen asleep before his eyes opened on a light—the little gliding moon shed by an electric torch. 'Are you all right, my dear? I thought I heard you call. I thought perhaps you wanted something.'

It was his Aunt Miranda.

'Or did you have a bad dream?'

A board creaked. The small moon lurched nearer, its shaft falling across his clothes on a chair. Suddenly the door was flung open, the ceiling light switched on. His grandmother stood on the threshold. 'Miranda! Are you walking in your sleep?'

'I thought I heard Johnnie call out.'

'Did you call?' his grandmother asked, turning to him.

'Not that I know of. I don't think I called.'

'Is there anything you want?'

'No, no! I've got everything I want, everything, thank you.'

'Well, then—we'll leave you alone. Quick march, Miranda!'

Motionless, she watched Miranda trail out of the room. Shutting the door on her, she advanced to his bedside. 'Are you sure you're all right, Johnnie?' All the bark and briskness had gone out of her manner; she seemed to be imploring him to feel a little unwell, to need an aspirin or a clean handkerchief.

'Perfectly all right, Grandmother. I'm sorry if I caused all this disturbance.' She stood there, looking down on him, and he suddenly became conscious of the lowness of his divan bed.

'Do you miss your mother, Johnnie?'

He hadn't been aware of missing his mother, but he knew he ought to say something appropriate. 'Well—yes, I suppose I do.'

She bent downwards, swaying and toppling. Spreading her hands on his pillow to support herself, she leaned closer and closer. The ends of her two short bristling pigtails descended on him. He blinked, and she settled her lips on his cheek in a long, delving kiss. 'There! That's from her.'

She was so breathless from the effort of stooping that he had to take her by the shoulders and push her upwards. But she walked firmly to the door, opened it, switched off the light, reappeared in silhouette. *'Fais dodo!'* she said in an artificial, chirruping voice, and closed the door gently behind her.

He pulled himself together as one does after a bad dream and almost immediately fell asleep again.

He slept so deeply that he woke not knowing where he was—only that it was broad day, and must be somewhere in the country, for a cuckoo was calling. Then he remembered the narrow valley and the pear trees blooming along its green windings. Though unforgettably lovely, it was only the beginning of his westward journey. He looked at his watch and saw he must get up at once if he were not to be late for breakfast and delayed in starting. He was half dressed when Woodie came in with a tray: porridge, sausages and bacon, marmalade—a real English breakfast. She set it on a table by the window and stayed to pour out his coffee. 'Will you be stopping for lunch?' she asked. He shook his head; and then interrogated her face. Her expression was sad and displeased. Perhaps she had cooked something special—he didn't want to slight her. 'Do you think I ought?'

'No, Master Johnnie. Much better not. The ladies ought to take things quietly today, after all the excitement of looking forward to you. They're not so young as they were. But they'll both be down to see you off.'

The garden was so filled with the scent and toss of daffodils, the ribes was so pink and resonant with bees, the sun shone so affectionately on the house and on the farewelling group—his grandmother and Aunt Miranda side by side, Woodie a little behind—and everything looked so exactly as it should, and so like Jane Austen in its gentle sprightliness, that he almost decided to change his mind and stay, as he was begged to do, for lunch. But little clouds were rising, the pure weather might not last, he did not want his first sight of the Welsh mountains to be checkered by a windscreen wiper—which anyhow did not work very well; so he said his goodbyes, and kissed them all, and promised to come again, and got into the car.

'*Bon voyage!*' cried his grandmother. It was the same false, chirruping sweetness of that '*Fais dodo!*' the night before.

'Good-by-ee!' he shouted, emphasizing its colonial heartiness and vulgarity, and started the car with a roar. That performance in his bedroom had somehow disgraced him. He wanted to get away and forget about it as soon as possible.

'A nice lad, didn't you think?' said Miranda, rather stiffly. 'A pity he didn't want to stay.'

The only acknowledgement of this was a brief, scornful laugh.

'Of course he was bored to extinction,' Miranda said. 'Never mind; he's done his duty by us. Duty done, cut and run.'

'I don't wonder he bolted, after the way you chased him,' said her sister. 'Leaping into the car to sit next to him, making eyes at him all through dinner, using that hideous old Bishop Mainwaring, who was no relation at all, as a pretext to get him to yourself—and then, when all else failed, sneaking into his bedroom, only waiting to put on your best dressing gown. Poor boy, no wonder he fled while he could!'

'I wished you had put on your best dressing gown, too. That old one is getting very shabby. And rather smelly—not to put too fine a point on it.'

Woodie stood in the kitchen, hearing their voices snap and snarl as they tore at each other's self-respect. They quarrelled continually—it helped pass the time for them. But this quarrel was bound to be worse than usual, because of all the excitement and looking forward. They would get over it, though, poor old cats; there was nothing else they could do. Meanwhile, she must think about cooking lunch, and how best to dispose of the remains of that grand dinner—the big chicken, the expensive asparagus, all that cream. It wouldn't do to serve up the chicken cold, reminding them. *Rissoles* would be best; *rissoles* don't suggest anything out of the ordinary. And for the evening, an asparagus soup and some creamed rice.

Johnnie slackened his foot on the accelerator. That first escaping burst of speed had rinsed his mind; now he could drive at his own pace, looking about him, following by-roads, stopping to admire. After a brief shower, the sun had come out again, brighter and more enhancing than ever. Trees seemed to be rushing into leaf; the bluebells that grew along the roadside made a perspective of sapphire. And there, shaping out of the distance and quite unmistakable, was Skirrid Fawr—the mountain that split asunder at the moment when Christ died on the Cross. The day was before him, and his own, and time was his to do what he pleased with, and he hadn't the slightest idea where he would spend the night.

# A JUMP AHEAD

W E had divorced in amity; when we met again after the statutory six months we found each other such good company that we agreed to go on meeting from time to time. As time went on, and we began to fall into our new ruts, these meetings inevitably lost their elasticity, became formalities of goodwill, obligations of good manners, and took place at longer and longer intervals. By tacit consent, too, we had come to avoid visiting each other's dwelling, and met on neutral ground. For me, this was a matter of regret since it deprived me of Mary's cooking or of my own. Restaurant cooking gives me indigestion.

At our last meeting Mary had been full of plans and excitement. Her great-aunt Barbara had died; minus some miserly bequests to servants and learned societies her estate, a considerable one, had come to Mary as residuary legatee. 'Barby's money won't know itself,' Mary boasted. 'There it sat, leading a quiet orderly life. I'm going to make it rattle.' And she showed me brochures of the luxury cruises she intended to go on.

I thought it probable that Mary would find a further husband on one of these cruises; and when the flights of picture postcards ceased (the last was from Reykjavic, which seemed an odd place to be luxurious in) I assumed this had happened, and that when I saw her again (if I ever saw her again) she would toss him at me as a *fait accompli*, remarking 'Michael's latest idea is to buy an opossum', before I had made sure of his existence—which would be in keeping with her habit of always being a jump ahead. It was also in keeping with Mary's habits that she should be married; and I thought of her as such till a small paragraph in an evening paper caught my eye. Then I learned that my stepson, Basil, had been charged with driving while drunk and that his mother, called to give evidence, still bore my name. She had moved to a new address, in a grander quarter. It was from that address, and about a twelve-month later, that she wrote to me, saying that it was years since we had met, that there was something she particularly wanted to ask me about, and when would I be in Inner London. I suggested a date, I invited her to lunch, I sent a suit to the cleaners; and on my way to the res taurant I bought her a box of *langues de chat*. I thought it had grown rather too late in the day for flowers. For that matter, it had grown rather late for another meeting. Almost seven years had gone by since the day she told me with such animation about Barby's money. Neither of us was likely to be improved by that lapse of time. She had travelled—but at the end of her travels she had come back to Basil, a depressing bourne. As for me, I had retired from being a mathematical coach and—as happens when one retires—had grown old.

To what extent I had grown old I did not realize till I saw Mary's start of surprise and her immediate assumption of a kind encouraging manner. In her, I saw no change. She had been middle-aged when last we met, and was middle-aged now. Only her hat was different. Then, it had been an inclined plane. Now it was an irregular cone. We sat down opposite each other at a small table, and were in no hurry to look each other in the face. Apparently Mary found the assumption of a kind encouraging manner inhibiting. I realized that talk must be kept up by me. While we drank our cocktails I asked her about her travels, about her fellow-travellers, about her new home, about her investments. I even asked about that oaf, Basil. And all my questions she answered diligently and carefully, and never once cut into what I was saying with some remark of her own. I drudged on with Basil. I had never imagined I should express so much interest in Basil. I thought I had squeezed him dry when another drop oozed out.

'Is Basil thinking of getting married?'

'I don't know. He goes out a great deal, but not in a marrying way.'

At that moment the waiter brought our asparagus, and we occupied ourselves with eating it, but Mary must have become mindful that it was now her turn to enquire, for presently she said, 'And what have you been doing, all this long while?'

'Growing old,' I replied.

'You're lucky to have the time to do it in.'

As of old, she had left me standing: all my topics, so nicely planned—my retirement, indications of my autobiography, my operation for a hernia, my acquisition of a tortoise with my reasons for calling him Runcorn—all were invalidated by that summary judgement that I had devoted seven undistracted years to growing old, and could afford to do so.

It seemed a poor return for my interest in Basil. But at least, it was better than kindness and encouragement. With luck, I thought, this unnatural lunch might yet be salvaged; we might yet scramble back onto our old terms and be well into a quarrel by the time I was eating *escalope de veau* and she Chicken Maryland. Probably all she needed was a little shove. Remembering that she had always been quick to react to a white wine, I ordered a *Pouilly Fuissé*.

'But, Gilbert, you don't like white wine. It doesn't agree with you.'

'One can only be old once,' I replied. It was the kind of quip I particularly dislike; but it served, for she laughed, and rubbed her cheeks as though to call her expression to life. And with the first glass she began to talk about growing old. She talked with a kind of pondering eloquence, as though it were a subject to which she had given a great deal of thought but only now was in a position to expound. Some of the things she said were silly, others were rather striking; but what illumined her words, and gave them character and consistency, was their tone of wistfulness and speculative appreciation. It was as though she were praising the scenery and perfect climate of some island which none of her cruises had allowed her to set foot on.

'Another thing that would be so marvellous would be knowing that, remember as you might, you wouldn't have to do anything about it—not make amends, find a new way round—nothing of that sort. Everything would have been put safely out of reach. Even with the most appalling things you had done, the most embarrassing mistakes, it would be like sitting on a mountain and seeing, far, far below you, a minute bull chasing a minute man. And the lovely things, they would be out of reach, too. You wouldn't have to cry your eyes out because you couldn't hold onto them much longer. You would . . .' It was unheard-of for Mary to talk like this, and I was listening with the touched astonishment with which parents see a quadruped baby suddenly stumble towards them on two feet, when it flashed on me that all this was part of her kind encouragement; that she was

45

gently shoe-horning me into my old age. 'Would!' I interrupted. 'Would! Why all these conditionals? It *would* be wonderful to be old. It *would* be wonderful to die. My dear girl, the word is "will", not "would". There's no conditional about it.'

She was like a snail drawing back its horns—alarmed, vulnerable and inoffensive. I have a liking for snails; they are beautiful, and rather intelligent. Seeing Mary draw back her horns, I regretted my interruption. It was a coarse act, for she had been enjoying her run of eloquence and doing me no harm. 'Tell me more about your travels,' I said. 'Tell me about Iceland.'

'I didn't like it. It frightened me. I don't mean those absurd geysers. But it's like a horse's skull, and it hates you.'

There was real fear in her eyes. She whisked it away, and again asked me what I had been doing with myself. This time I told her about my operation, and about the tortoise, and the upheaval of a retirement, and consulted her about redecorating my ground-floor flat—retirement had given me leisure enough to realize how dirty it was, and how inconvenient. As usual, her advice was excellent. She found room for my besetting books by turning the larder I never use into a book-closet, and her flawless memory for dimensions and objects enabled her to rearrange my dwelling as though she had been in it only yesterday. My own memory is far from flawless, and I took out my pocket-book and made notes of what she said while our pudding plates were taken away and our coffee brought.

'Thank you,' I said. 'Thank you very much, Mary. And now what about you? Wasn't there something you wanted to ask me?'

'Yes. I want you to be my executor.'

'Your executor? But why? And why me? You know me well enough to know I'd be hopeless.'

'You'd be all right if you were put to it. Besides, my solicitor will be the other, he will do the practical dealings. All I want you for is to tear up letters, and generally dispose of my private life, and see that various things I've left to people really get to them.'

And fend off Basil, I thought. It was an inducement; but not a sufficient one.

'It's flattering that you should remember how good I am at parcels,' I said. 'My single talent well employed, I did them better than you. But I won't be your executor, my dear. For one thing, an executor has to be a survivor—and I shall be dead long before you are.'

'Don't be so sure of that.'

An instant later, deftly and deliberately, she knocked over her coffee-cup. A look that was almost a look of criminality was recast to match exclamations about clumsiness, and apologies to the waiter, who came and mopped.

'So you will let me put you in?' she resumed when he had gone. 'I am so grateful. I can't tell you what a weight off my mind it is.'

'You can't jump me like that,' I said. 'I want to know what *is* on your mind. Mary, what is all this? What did you mean, just before you knocked over your cup so cleverly?'

'What I said.'

'You're fifteen years younger than I am, you're wearing a new hat, you look the picture of health. . . . You've got some nonsense into your head.'

'That's all you know.'

She put on her teasing smile; but now the look of criminality was that of a criminal brazening it out.

'Mary.'

'Oh, shut up, Gilbert! You bore me. Let's talk about something else.'

'I'd rather you told me,' I said after a pause.

'Leukaemia. That's why.'

I knew I could say nothing to comfort her. I told her I was sorry, and that I would be her executor if she wished. In my maladroit consternation I used the word 'gladly'. She laughed delightedly. I should not be needed for some time, she said; perhaps not for another year; she wanted to get things settled well beforehand, that was all. After I had put her into a taxi and waved a farewell, I remembered how I had interrupted her wistful evocation of growing old.

# FENELLA

'MAMMA!'

'Oh, do you know the Sackrees, too? Then I expect you know their cousins, the Leighs—Nicholl and Tabby Leigh. No? Oh, but you should! They've got such an amusing house.'

'Mamma!'

'At Margate, of all places, embossed with shells. Yes, Fenella, what is it?'

'Mamma, if you have no other plans for this afternoon, may I go to Grifone with Miss Wilson?'

'But I thought you were going to play tennis with Roger.'

'I was. But now he doesn't want to.'

'Tiresome boy! Well, darling, why not wait a little, and then we'll go and bathe in the lake together.'

'I bathed this morning. Twice. I bathed with the Darnleys, and then I bathed all over again with Susan and Melissa. Now I feel I want a change.'

'But, my pet, Grifone is halfway up the mountain, and just another of these squalid little villages with open drains. Anyway, why Grifone?'

'Miss Wilson is painting the church.'

The lady who didn't know the Leighs gave a laugh. 'Fenella wants a change after all that modern art at the Biennale.'

Fenella's mother echoed the laugh. 'Some good old English fare. Cut off the joint and two veg.'

'Oh, cruel! But I'm sure it's a perfect description.'

Both ladies laughed. Fenella remained silent and un-complyingly grave. All that money spent on having her teeth straightened, and never a smile out of her, thought her mother; and said 'Well, darling, I see you're bent on it. Go with my blessing. But don't hang over the drains. And for God's sake don't let Miss Wilson give you an ice off a barrow.'

'No, Mamma.'

She would be almost pretty, thought the lady who didn't know the Leighs, if she didn't look so like a tallow candle, and hadn't her father's upper lip. But a miss is as good as a mile—and in this case it was a mile. The object of these considerations having moved away, she said, 'All the same, I expect your daughter's right. The young have an instinct for what's coming next, and ten to one in another few years we shall all be scrambling to buy strong beefy canvases by Miss Wilson.'

'God forbid! Do you really think so?'

'I'm positive. After all, people are doting on Landseer already.'

'Landseer, yes. I'm beginning to dote on him myself. But Miss Wilson.'

'Sh-h-h! There she is.'

A tall lean woman in a faded blue cotton dress and carrying an easel had come up the steps of the hotel terrace. Fenella hurried towards her. 'It's all right, I can come. I'll just dash to my room and put on my rope-soles.'

'Dash, then!' exclaimed Miss Wilson in a voice too loud and too dramatic to sound convincing.

The two ladies averted their gaze and lowered their voices.

'Doesn't it seem extraordinary to find someone like that in San Barbaro?'

'Quite extraordinary.'

To Miss Wilson, on the other hand, who had settled in San Barbaro twelve years before, and so matter-of-factly that in another twelve years she would probably be regarded as an inhabitant, it was the presence of such figures as Fenella's parents, the lady who didn't know the Leighs, the Darnleys, etc., that seemed extraordinary.

In point of fact, they had got there by a very natural course of events. In 1956, Timon Hogg, an eminent art critic and connoisseur, had an attack of mumps on his way home from Venice. His wife, his sister-in-law and his nephew, who were travelling with him, had known instantaneously what to do, and battered their way into a convent near Belluno, assuring the mother superior that in England everyone of distinction, regardless of denomination, went into convents for nursing. The onslaught was so pervasive and Timon's Italian so commandingly fluent that the mother superior gave way. To visit the sick is a Christian obligation; perhaps she thought that to accept visitations by the sick came under the same heading. Anyway, they got in. They were soon on terms of affection with the whole convent, and giving a great deal of trouble. Finally, the convent's doctor and the chaplain intervened. What the convalescent needed, said the doctor, was pure air and repose. Pure air and repose were available in perfection, together with mountain scenery, said the chaplain, in his native village of San Barbaro, where the church contained some most interesting frescoes, where the policeman's wife, a retired nurse, let lodgings that were simple but commodious and entirely free from insects. Somehow or other, the party was bundled off to San Barbaro. What was left of the frescoes appeared to have been painted in mid-nineteenth century by the village idiot, and the lodgings stank of disinfectant and rang with mosquitoes. But Timon, never at a loss for an unknown masterpiece, discovered in the loft above the sacristy two icons and a harpsichord decorated by Angelica Kauffmann, and drew attention to them in an article. From then on, San Barbaro became a preserve of Timon's intimate circle, who came there on their way to the Biennale or on their way back, arriving in punctual flocks like migrant birds. A stretch of the lakeside at a discreet remove from the outfall of the village's main drain was cleared of its deposit of old tins, old shoes, old tires and broken crockery, a tennis court was laid out, and two rival hotels were built and promoted by Signora Amalia Pons, widow.

'Height,' remarked Miss Wilson, leaning over the wall at the third turn of the road that led to Grifone, 'height shows one proportion.'

'Yes, doesn't it,' gasped Fenella. She was already rather out of breath, which was why they had paused. The proportion Miss Wilson had in mind was that between the old San Barbaro and the new. Seen from above, this was reassuring. The Excelsior and the Splendide were well on the outskirts of the village; round its patron's mild dome, nothing broke the pattern of tiled roofs, the outdoor-apricot-coloured roofs over which the shadow of the mountain would presently advance its astonishing blue.

'From here the roofs look almost like corrugated iron,' Fenella said.

'Rested?' inquired Miss Wilson. 'Shall we go on?'

Two designs warred in Miss Wilson's mind. She wanted

to get to Grifone and finish her painting of the church; she wanted to make a portrait of this pale, lanky girl, with her air of being a mermaid who had never for an instant sported in her native element. But Grifone must come first. The girl was hers for the whole afternoon. Not so the light.

Fenella was more simply preoccupied with self-expression, idealism and revenge; she wanted to show those bores, those tittering, copycatting, running-around-in-a-circle-and-being-fashionable bores, that she, at any rate, could discern the difference between the sham and the true. While they were all laughing at Miss Wilson and her easel; while Miss Wilson, sitting like Coleridge 'in the exceeding lustre and the pure intense irradiation' of her love of art, was paying no attention to any of them, Fenella had defied public opinion and made determined approaches —had asked the name of a flower, had offered an ice, had asked to see her pictures. 'What I would actually like would be to see you actually painting,' she had then said. The invitation to Grifone had followed; and having lied all round, and plotted like a Communist, and endured two dreary strategic bathes in one morning she was now on the way to enjoy it. Unfortunately, the road to Grifone was remorselessly steep, gritty, parchingly hot and apparently interminable; and all that bathing had weakened her legs. Nothing had weakened Miss Wilson's legs. Despite the easel and the canvas and the knapsack, they darted on ahead. It was like following a machine—one, two, one two!—a reaping machine or something of that sort.

Though the mountainside from below looked uninhabited, they passed several farmhouses, where large dogs rushed out at them, where unseen pigs yelled. At the roadside by one of these farms a terrible sort of idiot with an enormous head lay in a go-cart under a cloud of flies. Miss Wilson's legs darted onwards. 'Nearly there, Fenella.'

'Oh, good.'

'In winter this road is often impassable for weeks on end.'

'Really? How do the—the *Grifonesi* get out?'

'They don't.'

The flies that had buzzed over the idiot seemed to be buzzing in Fenella's head. The stony surface of the road was so hot that it was like walking over red-hot plough-shares.

'If I lived at Grifone, I think I should quite look forward to winter,' she said.

'What? I didn't hear.'

'I just said that must be a gorgeous view from Grifone.'

Presently, remarking that this was a short cut to the church, Miss Wilson stepped over a dead snake, scrambled up a precipice and was out of sight. Struggling up the narrow path between the brambles, Fenella was obsessed with a fear that she would slip, roll to the bottom, lie there beside the snake and be swarmed over by the ants that were swarming over it.

The church squatted in an enclosure of long sunburned grasses. Here and there black wire crosses rose out of the grass like thistles. It was a very small church and quite ordinary, except for the porch, which was disproportionately ample and deep. Miss Wilson had already set up her easel, the canvas was mounted, and she was standing back surveying it with a thoughtful expression.

'Please, may I look?' Fenella asked.

Miss Wilson made way for her. Fenella's first impression

was disconcerting. Miss Wilson, after all, was only another of these clever modern artists. Yet the picture did not seem to be altogether an abstract: it looked more like a church the wrong way up.

'Oh, but I *like* it!' She had not wanted to sound like Mamma, but the words came automatically, and she did.

'You haven't seen it yet. I was standing it on its head to see how it hangs together.' Miss Wilson reversed the canvas. It now looked exactly like the church.

'I *see*.'

This sounded even more reminiscent of Mamma. She blushed furiously.

Miss Wilson glanced up from unpacking the knapsack. 'My poor child, how hot you look! Why don't you go and sit in the church, and cool off?' At that moment Fenella had no mermaid charms for her, was not paintable, was not even pitiable—an affected chit.

Dogged by her mother's voice, dogged, too, by the thought that the long grasses must certainly harbour a great many snakes whose hissings would be inaudible in that din of grasshoppers, and reflecting on the inadequacy of all human relationships—she was not really cynical but there are some things one just has to admit—Fenella approached the church. The shade in the porch was as blinding as the sun outside. Beneath her tread there was suddenly a rattling, resounding vacancy, crossed by vacillating iron slats. She drew back.

'Go on, go on! It's only to keep out animals,' Miss Wilson called.

Inside the church was silence, coolness, safety, a smell of piety and paraffin, a dimmed daylight. A small lamp steadfastly burned in a crimson glass shade. Fenella made a deep genuflection, crossed herself, spread her handkerchief on the floor, crossed herself again and went down on her knees. Only then did she remember an omission: dry crossings of oneself are comparatively worthless. She ventured back into the porch, reawakened the rattling and the vacancy, found a holy-water stoup. 'She can't be coming out already!' muttered Miss Wilson.

Properly dampened, like linen before ironing, Fenella returned to the handkerchief and settled down to go on resolving to become a Roman Catholic. Of course, it wasn't totally original—Peregrine Fielding had, and Lucy Trivett, and Mr. Walmisley. But in her case it would be different. They were all middle-aged—Mr. Walmisley was over forty, indeed, and could remember Queen Mary's toques; their lives were behind them. She was thirteen. Her passions were stronger than theirs, her need intenser. She wanted to escape from always feeling scornful, selfish and lonely. She wanted to have a deep spiritual life that wouldn't always be leaking away from her. She craved to be understood and guided and rebuked and consoled and to feel herself part of an all-embracing yet exclusively True Church. She longed to call someone Father—someone not Popski. If she could get inside—walk calmly and firmly over all the rows and arguments and amusement and expostulation as she had walked over the arrangement in the porch to keep out animals, and be christened all over again, and properly, with salt and holding a candle in her hand, and be called Chantal instead of horrid Fenella, like an advertisement of pyjamas! But no one would possibly listen to her. No one ever listened to one unless one said the wrong thing. If she could have a vision . . . or if at this moment a priest would come into the church, a dear simple old parish priest who wouldn't laugh at her bad Italian . . . or if Miss Wilson were a Roman Catholic, and also rather different, so that one wouldn't have that Hunt-the-Thimble sensation. As for Peregrine, or Lucy, or Mr. Walmisley, that was quite out of the question. They were bogus. Anyone with an atom of religious feeling could see that.

Meanwhile time was running away, whirling past her like a cloud of dust. In three days, they would be driving home. In a week, she would be back at school, struggling with algebra, flinching at lacrosse, showing off about all the famous people her parents knew, reading poetry in the W.C. A vision! She must pray for a vision. She shut her eyes, clenched her fists till the nails ran into her palms and prayed so intensely that she felt perfectly hollow. A vision —or perhaps a voice. The voiceless blood rang in her ears. When she opened her eyes, nothing was there. Presently she realized that she was deathly cold. I am going to faint, she thought, and revised this to, I am going into a trance. But she merely went on feeling extremely cold and bruised all over. She got up and staggered about the church on legs that did not seem like her own. Her heart, too, had become cold.

She observed as impartially as though she were following a guide round yet another *palazzo* that the building was poverty-stricken and decaying, that the Stations of the Cross were oleographs in Oxford frames, that the altar frontal had been patched with red flannel, that there was a pro-fusion of blood and the usual awful statues. Near the second altar, on a table covered with a green baize cloth, lay a long narrow box with a glass top and sides, like a showcase, containing some she-saint or other dressed in sky-blue satin with a great deal of lace and puffings and furbelows. The figure was about two-thirds life size, but yards and yards of satin must have been expended in the puffings and furbelows. On her head was a wreath of white roses, her face was covered with some sort of dingy kid, and she had yellowish kid gloves on her hands. When she was new, she must have been very smart, and the height of fashion. Even now, Grifone must think quite a lot of her, for there were several bouquets of artificial flowers on the table and a candlestand near by. Fenella had not brought her purse so she could not honourably light a candle. Yet, having thought of it, it seemed impolite not to do so. Miss Wilson had said something about drinking goat's milk on a terrace overlooking the view, so she must have some money about her. Fenella went rather slowly towards the door, nerving herself to borrow the price of a candle. She noticed the handkerchief, still lying where she had knelt down to pray—so hopefully, so desperately, and now seeming so long ago. She picked it up, saw from its condition how right she had been to spread it between her knees and the floor. In the next breath she was racing back to the glass box. Had she not prayed for a vision? A vision might take any form, might arise from the most unpromising, the most rubbishy lair. She would light all the candles as an Act of Faith and pray all over again, and this time the vision would be granted; the face would smile or a gloved hand would lift and beckon.

There were eight candles—her unlucky number; but never mind, that was only superstition. She had placed three candles when it occurred to her that she would give a little polish to the glass lid of the box. It must have been very devoutly breathed on; dry rubbing did no good at all.

She spat on her handkerchief; the grime began to come off in little rolls. Spitting and rubbing, breathing and polishing, she became so absorbed in her attentions to the glass that she did not glance at what lay beneath it until she had cleaned down as far as the hands folded on the rosary. What extraordinary gloves—so thin that the nails, long, and rather dirty, showed through. No kid could be so thin, no silk could fit so closely. Chicken skin? No, it must be wax. The hands were made of wax, that in course of time had yellowed and grown dry. She looked at the face. It had blue glass eyes, to match the blue dress. One of them projected from the face, squeezed out by the shrivelling socket into which it had been fitted. It seemed to stare at her with alarm. The other eye was still in place, and placid. She was looking at a small dead body, dressed in blue satin, with a lace veil falling from under a wreath of white rosebuds and a few grains of rouge adhering to its cheeks. Too small to be a woman, too overdressed to be a child, it lay on a white satin mattress and did not even look dead. It looked like death's doll.

Setting her teeth, she lit the three candles, and ran for her life. She leaped over the rattling pit, she was out in the sun, propping herself against the entrance of the porch. 'Stay just as you are!' shouted Miss Wilson.

Chit or no chit, the girl was certainly a born model. As though the words had nailed her, she remained exactly as she had been when they were spoken, no hand sneaking up to her hair, no redressing shift of balance, no change of expression even. It was an interesting pose, too, with that El Greco quality of artless, outrageous drama that one only sees in the adolescent. The ballerina expansion of her sulphur-yellow skirt would have to be lopped into a more rational shape—but its colour was just what was wanted to pick up the patches of lichen on the church roof. Well, she hadn't come to Grifone for nothing, this young person.

'Thank you. Dis-miss!' Looking up from her canvas, Miss Wilson saw that the girl was still holding that remarkable pose. She couldn't have heard. 'Thank you, Fenella. That's all. I've done with you.'

The girl undid herself from the wall—there was really no other word for it—and came slowly through the grasses and the clattering grasshoppers. Her head drooped, and once she put her hand up to it as though to support a suddenly felt weight. That was a good pose, too. It was to be hoped that she hadn't got a sunstroke.

'Well, did you enjoy your rest in the church? Did you see the saint?'

'The Saint?'

'In the glass case. Didn't you notice her?'

'Yes. Is she a saint? She looks sort of Ninetyish.'

'Eighteen eighty-three. She was the daughter of a local landowner—a girl about your age. Very devout, and died of whooping cough.'

'Poor thing.'

'The mountain people were sure she was a saint. They even tried to get her taken up by the Vatican. Nothing came of it. But she's still called the Saint of Grifone, and there's still quite a cult of her—though not what it was, of course.'

'She's very small—if she was my age.'

'Girls were smaller then. No fresh air, no exercise.'

'Perhaps she's shrunk. Was it because she was a saint that they stuffed her—or whatever it was they did to make her keep?'

'No, no. That was her father. He was devoted to her, and very rich, so he had her embalmed.'

'Oh yes, of course! That's the word. I couldn't remember it. Miss Wilson, I'm afraid I ought to be getting back. I promised Mamma not later than six, and it's past that already.'

'Well, have a look at yourself in my painting first.'

The girl looked. Her face fell, and she instantly began to praise the colouring.

'But how will you get it back? Won't the flies settle on it?'

'If you don't mind carrying the easel.'

Some of the dead snake was still there but the idiot had been taken indoors. At intervals Miss Wilson remarked on Fenella's talent for keeping a pose and expressed an increasingly firm intention to paint a portrait of her.

'But why? I'm so wishy-washy. At my school they call me Creamed Rice.'

'You've got rather an interesting bone structure. Suppose we say tomorrow afternoon? I shan't keep you long for a first sitting.'

'But I'm afraid there won't be time. We're leaving early on Friday.'

'I can get all I want in a couple of hours, and work it up later.'

'And then there will be all sorts of farewell parties. I don't know what Mamma hasn't arranged.'

They parted outside the hotel. Fenella rushed upstairs, heard bath water running, hammered on the door.

'Mamma, Mamma! It's been too awful. Oh, for pity's sake, turn off that tap! Mamma! She's put me into her painting of the church—and made my poor skirt look like

a drowned rat. And now she's determined to paint a portrait of me. You must, *must* get me out of it!'

'I'll think it over. Mind, I don't promise.'

'But, Mamma! Her painting was grisly. Like a railway
poster.'

'You don't know everything, Fenella. Some people
think she's definitely good.'

'Good? They must be raving.'

'In any case, it will do you no harm to sit. And later on
it might turn out to be quite worth having.'

'But, Mamma, she's positively extinct. She's a living
corpse, she's . . .'

'I can't hear you,' her mother said, turning on the taps.

# HEATHY LANDSCAPE
WITH DORMOUSE

'WELL, Leo, dear—here we are, all settled and comfortable!' Mrs. Leslie, sitting on the ground, removed a
couple of burrs from her stocking and looked round on a
flattish expanse of heath. 'What heaven! Not a soul in
sight.' As though reinforcing this statement, an owl hooted
from a clump of alders.

People born into the tradition of English country life
are accustomed to eccentric owls. Mrs. Leslie and her
daughter Belinda accepted the owl with vaguely acknow-
ledging smiles. Her son-in-law, Leo Cooper, a Londoner
whose contacts with nature had been made at the very
expensive pleasure resorts patronized by his very rich
parents, found midday hoots disconcerting, and almost
said so. But did not, as he was just then in a temper and
wholly engaged in not showing it.

He was in a temper for several reasons, all eminently
adequate. For one thing, he had had a most unsatisfactory
night with Belinda; for another, impelled by the nervous
appetite of frustration he had eaten a traditional country
breakfast and it was disagreeing with him; for yet another,
he had been haled out on yet another of his mother-in-law's
picnics; finally, there was the picnic basket. The picnic
basket was a family piece, dating, as Mrs. Leslie said on its
every appearance, from an age of footmen. It was the
size of a cabin trunk, built for eternity out of red wicker,

equipped with massy cutlery and crockery; time had sharpened its red fangs, and however Leo took hold of it, they lacerated him. Also it caused him embarrassment to be seen carrying this rattling, creaking monstrosity, and today he had carried it farther than usual. The car was left where the track crossed a cattle bridge, and from there Mrs. Leslie staggered unerringly over a featureless stretch of rough ground to the exact place where they always picnicked because it was there that Belinda as a little girl had found a dormouse.

'Yes, it was just here—by these particular whin bushes. Do you remember, darling? You were five.'

'I thought I was six.'

'No, five. Because Uncle Henry was with us that day, and next year he had that gun accident—God rest his soul!'

Having crossed herself with a sigh, and allowed time for the sigh's implications to sink in, Mrs. Leslie pulled the picnic basket towards her and began fidgeting at the straps. 'Let me!' exclaimed Leo, unable to endure the intensified creakings, and at the same moment Belinda said, 'I will'

She did—with the same negligent dexterity she showed in every activity but the act of love. Out came the plates and the cutlery and the mugs and the home-made ginger beer and the paste sandwiches and the lettuce sandwiches and the hard-boiled eggs; out came the cakes they had specially stopped to buy at Unwin the grocer's, because his old aunt made them and it was so nice and right of him to let her feel useful still. Out, too, a few minutes later, came the ants and the flies and those large predatory bluebottles that materialize from solitary places like depraved desert fathers.

'Brutes! Go away! How Delia used to swear at blue-bottles! Poor Delia, I miss her to this day.'

'Leo will think we have a great many dead relations,' said Belinda. She glanced at him—a friendlier glance; as if she had temporarily forgotten who he was, thought Leo, and was ready to give him the kindness one extends to a stranger.

'We've got a whole new live one now,' said her mother. 'We've got Leo.'

The glance hardened to a stare. Replaced in his role of husband, he appealed no longer. 'There's that owl again,' he said. 'Is it usual for owls to hoot by day? Isn't it supposed to be a bad omen?'

'Frightfully.' Belinda's voice was so totally expressionless that it scalded him like an insult. He said with studied indifference, 'Never mind! I expect it's too late to do anything about it.'

She continued to stare at him and he stared back into her unreceiving eyes. Clear and round and wide-set, Belinda's eyes had the fatalistic melancholy of the eyes of hunting cats. Seeing her as a caged puma, silent, withdrawn in a stately sulk, turning her back on the public and on the bars of her cage, he had fallen in love with her at first sight. 'Belinda Leslie . . . Better look while you may; it's your only chance. She's in London for a week, being a bridesmaid, and then she'll go back to live with her widowed Mamma in a mouldering grange, and never get out again. She's one of those sacrificial daughters. . . . I believe the North of England's full of them.' A month later, she had snatched at his offer of marriage as though it were a still warm partridge; yes, exactly as though it were a still warm partridge—snatching the meat, ignoring the hand.

So wild for liberty, he thought; later, she will love. But halfway through their honeymoon she insisted on pining for home, on pining for her mother even, so they travelled back to Snewdon and were welcomed as both her dear children by Mrs. Leslie. Before I get away, he thought, and later on revised this to: if ever I get away, she will have sewn labels of 'Leo Leslie' on all my underclothes. Yet he felt a sneaking liking for her; she was always polite to him, and he was young.

Since then, three appalling weeks had passed. The weather was flawless; gooseberries appeared at every meal. There was no male society except for the deaf-and-dumb gardener and two rams who pastured on the former tennis court. They went nowhere except for picnics in the neighbourhood. Every picnicking place had associations. If he tried to escape the associations by suggestions of going farther afield in his swifter car, this merely provoked other picnics and more of the rattles and joltings of the family conveyance. And all the time things were as bad as ever between him and Belinda, and the only alleviation in their relationship was that he was now beginning to feel bored by it.

'I suppose that owl is an old admirer of yours. When does he produce the small guitar? After dark?' (For a little time, because of her melancholy, merciless eyes, he had called her Pussy.)

'I loathe Lear.'

'Darling!' To soften the rebuke in her voice, Mrs. Leslie offered her daughter a hard-boiled egg, which was rejected. Turning to Leo, she said, 'Belinda and I do a lot of bird watching. We get such interesting migrants here—quite unexpected ones, sometimes.'

Belinda gave a brief, wounding laugh.

'Blown off their course, I suppose,' said Leo. 'I see I must learn about birds.'

'Oh, you should! It makes such a difference. There have been times when they were really my only support. Of course, I have always loved them. Quite the first book I remember is *The History of the Robins*. Flapsy, Pecksy—what were the others called? By Mrs. Trimmer. Did you ever read it, Belinda?'

'No.'

Leo took out a slim note-book and wrote in it with a slender pencil. 'I'll make a note of the title. At last I may be able to give Belinda a book she hasn't read already.'

'How delicious lettuce sandwiches are!' Mrs. Leslie said. 'So much the most comfortable way of managing lettuces, don't you think, Leo?'

'Infinitely. Do you know that lettuce is a mild sedative?'

'Is it? I never knew that. Belinda, do have another lettuce sandwich.'

'No, thank you.'

'But only very mild,' continued Leo.

Belinda sprang to her feet, took a cigarette from her bag, lit it, and walked away.

'She never really cares for Unwin's cakes,' explained her mother. 'But do try one. You might.'

'Thank you. I'd love one.'

Apparently he was doomed to failure in his loves, for the cake tasted of sweat and cough linctus. He laid it down where presently he would be able to trample on it, and stared after Belinda. Mrs. Leslie noticed his stare.

'Belinda walks exactly like her father.'

'She walks beautifully.'

'Yes, doesn't she? I wonder where she's going.'

'She seems to be making for the car.'

'Perhaps she has left something in it. Or perhaps she wants to move it into the shade. She has always been so fond of it. She learned to drive it when she was twelve. Of course, yours is much newer. Is it an Austin, too?'

'A Bristol.'

'How nice!'

Belinda was certainly walking towards the car. Mrs. Leslie's ringed hand, clasping a half eggshell, began to crumple it. Hearing her gasp, he realized that she had been holding her breath. Belinda walked on. They watched her cross the cattle bridge and get into the car. They saw her start the car, turn it and drive away.

'So now they know.' Belinda spoke in the tone of one who has achieved some stern moral purpose. 'Or they soon will.'

Belinda was one of those fortunate persons who fly into a rage as though into a refrigerator. Walking across the heath in the glaring post-meridian sun she had felt a film of ice encasing her, armouring her from head to foot in sleekness and invulnerability. She felt, too, the smile on her lips becoming increasingly rigid and corpselike. When she got into the car, though it was hot as an oven she seemed to be adjusting the hands of a marble effigy on the wheel. The car's smell, so familiar, so much part of her life, waylaid her with its ordinary sensuality, besought her to have a good cry. But righteousness sustained her. She turned the car and drove away, taking a studied pleasure in steering so skilfully among the ruts and ridges of the cart track. The track ran out into a lane, the car began to travel smoothly, she increased speed. The whole afternoon was before her;

she could go where she pleased. The whole afternoon was also before Leo and her mother, and a wide range of reflections; for there on the heath, with not a soul in sight, they would have to remain till she drove back to collect them. When would that be? Not till she had forgiven them. And that would not be until she had forgotten them, forgotten their taunts and gibes and the silly smirks they had exchanged, making a party against her, looping their airy conversation over her silence—as though she were a child sulking in a corner. Well, they could practise airy conversation, sitting there on the heath with the picnic basket. Presently the conversation would falter, they would be forced to speculate, to admit, to learn their lesson. Slow scholars, they would be allowed plenty of time for the lesson to sink in.

With the whole afternoon before her, and in a landscape as familiar to her as the shrubberies of her birthplace, she drove with elegance through a network of lanes and lesser lanes, turning aside to skirt round villages or houses where someone in a gateway might recognize her. Once, she got out of the car and watched through a gap in a laurel hedge a charitable fête that was being held on the lawn beyond. There were the stalls, with their calico petticoats flapping; there were the little tables, and the enlisted schoolchildren bringing tea on trays, there were the ladies of the locality and their daughters. How dowdy they looked, and how cheerful! Six months ago, she had been quite as dowdy and quite often cheerful too; but now the secret was lost, never again would she wear a small floral pattern with a light heart. Dowdy, cheerful, dutiful and self-satisfied—that was the lot appointed for Belinda Leslie. And if she had had a living father, or a brother, a decent allowance, a taste for religion or blood sports, or had been sent to a secretarial college—any alternative to Mother's swaddle of affection, fidget and egotism—she might have accepted the lot appointed and been at this moment at one of the little tables, agreeing that raspberries were really nicer than strawberries: a reflection made by all when the strawberry season is over. But to get away from Mother she had married Leo, who was so much in love with her and whom she immediately didn't love; and then to get away from Leo, and with nowhere else to run to, she had run home. Somehow it had not occurred to her that Leo would come too. For the first few days, he had stalked about being intolerably uncivil to his hostess. Then there had been that ghastly bedroom quarrel, the worst they had ever had. The next day, Mother, smelling the blood of his misery, had settled on him, assiduously sucking, assiduously soothing, showing him old snapshots and making him one of the family. And Leo, who had started up in her life as a sort of mother-slaying St. George, lay down like a spaniel to be tickled, and like a spaniel snarled at her from under Mother's skirts. Well, the one-of-the-family process could be continued on the heath. There would be touchingly comic stories about little Belinda, a sweet child really, but perhaps a trifle spoilt, needing a firmer hand. . . . Mrs. Whitadder and old Miss Groves at the table nearest the laurel hedge were startled to hear a car they hadn't known was there being so impetuously driven away.

In a landscape as familiar to her as the shrubberies of her birthplace Belinda found she had managed to mislay the turning beyond Upton All Saints and was temporarily lost. This, while it lasted, was quieting and dreamlike. The high road banks, bulky with late-summer growth, with scabious and toadflax and hemp agrimony, closed her in. Silvery, waning, plumed grasses brushed against the car, swish-swish; smells of unseen wheat, of turnips and once of a fox, puffed in at the open window. She passed a pair of cottages, brick-built and of surpassing ugliness, called, as one would expect, 'Rose' and 'Coronation'. A baker's van stood in front of them, and the baker and Mrs. Coronation were conversing across the garden fence. It would be childish in the extreme to imagine herself into that woman's shoes, with Mr. Leo Coronation coming placidly home from a day's work to eat a substantial meat tea in his shirtsleeves and then go off to spend the evening at the pub—unless he did a little twilight gardening. She managed not to imagine this, and drove on and soon after approached the cottages, the baker's van and the conversation once more, having driven in a circle. Quieting and dreamlike though this might be, if she persevered in it the conversation would begin to feel itself being hurried to a close. So this time she turned to the left, and, coming to a road post, consulted it. Billerby & Frogwick. She was much farther east than she supposed. Yet she could have known it, for in the very faint haze spreading over the eastern sky one could read the sea. It was still a beautiful, endless summer afternoon; the shadows of the whin bushes and the clump of alders could be left to lengthen for a long time yet while Mother and Leo got to know each other better and better. Having forgotten them sufficiently to have to remember them she was nearer forgiving them. They had looked so very silly, sitting on the hot heath and toying with Unwin's uneatable cakes. By now they would be looking even sillier. The longer she left them there, the better she would be to endure seeing them again. Billerby & Frogwick. It was beyond Billerby that a track off the road to Frogwick ran past a decoy wood and between fields of barley and of rye to the barn that stood on the sea wall and had once been a church. Years ago, exploring on her bicycle, she had found the barn, and talked with the old man who was sheltering there from the rain; and even then had known better than to report it. 'Time of the Danes,' he had said, looking cautiously out across the saltings, as if the Danes might be coming round the corner in their long-beaked ships. 'Or thereabouts.' 'But how do you know it was a church?' 'Course it were a church. What prove it—that there door ain't never been shut.' Not wanting to endanger her find, she never went back to it.

Sure enough, the door was open. There were two farm workers in the barn, tinkering at a reaper. She heard one say to the other, 'Tighten her up a bit, and that will be all.' So she went and sat on the wall's farther side, listening for the last clink of their spanners. They came out not long after, had a look at the car, called it a rum old Methusalem, and went away on motor bicycles. But she continued to sit on the slope of the wall, listening to the grasshoppers and watching the slow, ballet-postured mating of two blue butterflies. If you brush them apart, they die; yet from their fixed, quivering pattern they seem to be in anguish. Probably they don't feel much either way. It was then that she became aware of what for a stupid moment she thought to be a cuckoo, a disembodied, airy tolling of two notes, somewhere out to sea. But it was a bell buoy, rocking and ringing. It seemed as though a heart were beating—a serene, impersonal heart that rocked on a tide of salt water.

The breeze dropped, the music was silenced; but the breeze would resume, the heart begin to beat again. She sat among the grasshoppers, listening, so still that a grasshopper lit on her hand. All along the wall the yellow bedstraw was in bloom, its scent and colour stretching away on either side like a tidemark of the warm, cultivatable earth. If the silly Leslies had held on to their farmlands, it would be fun, uneconomic but fun, to take in another stretch of saltings: to embank and drain it, to sluice the salt out of it, to watch the inland weeds smothering glasswort and sea lavender, and bees adventuring, warm and furry, where little crabs had sidled along the creeks; then to plough, to sow, to reap the first, terrific harvest. But no one did that sort of thing nowadays. The sea continued to retreat, and the farmers to squat behind the wall and complain of the cost of its upkeep. There was that cuckoo again—no, that bell buoy. She addressed herself in a solemn voice: 'If you sit here much longer, you will fall asleep.' Exerting herself to sit erect, she heeled over and fell asleep.

Once, she stirred towards consciousness, and thought the Danes had arrived. Opening one eye, she caught sight of her yellow silk trousers, reasoned that the Danes could not possibly arrive when she was dressed like this and was asleep again. When next she woke, a different arrival had taken place. The sea mist had come inland, was walking in swathes over the saltings, had silenced the grasshoppers, extinguished the sun. Her blissful, Leo-less sleep was over. She was back in real life again, compelled to look at her wristwatch in order to see how long she had possessed her anonymity. It was past eight. Good God!—Mother and Leo on the heath!

She snatched up her bag and ran. Because she was in a

hurry, the car wouldn't start. When it did, it baulked and hesitated. Just before the decoy, it stopped dead. It had run out of petrol.

It was useless to repine; she must leave the car on the marsh, as earlier in the day she had left Mother and Leo on the heath. Obviously, it was the kind of day when one leaves things. Billerby could not be more—at any rate, not much more—than four miles away; though it was a small village, it must be able to produce a gallon of petrol and a man to drive her out to the decoy. If not, she could ring up a garage. Walking briskly, she could reach Billerby in not much over an hour—once on the road, she might even get a lift. By half past nine at the latest . . . She stopped; a stone had got into her shoe, a thought had darted into her head. By half past nine those two would have finished their dinner, would be drinking coffee and wondering when foolish Belinda would come home, bringing her tail behind her. For of course, they had not remained on the heath. Mother would have sent Leo to look for a man. 'I think we ought to look for a man' was how she would have expressed it. And Leo, urban ignoramus though he was, would eventually have found one. Yes, they were all right. There was no call to waste pity on them. It was she who was cold and footsore and hungry and miles from home. Miles from home, and at least two miles from Billerby, and faint with hunger! Now that she had begun to think how hungry she was, she could think of nothing else. Two paste sandwiches, half a lettuce sandwich—Oh, why had she rejected that hard-boiled egg? Beasts! Gibing, guzzling beasts! By the time she walked into Billerby, Belinda was hating her husband and her mother as vehemently as when she walked away, leaving them on the heath.

But not with such righteous calm and elation. Her first sight of Billerby showed her that it would have been better to go to Frogwick. There was no inn. There was no filling station. There was a post office, but it was duly closed in accordance with government regulations. There were two small shops. One of them was vacant and for sale, the other appeared to sell only baby clothes. Nowhere held out the smallest promise of being able to produce a gallon of petrol. As for a man who would drive her, there was no man of any sort. At one moment there had been three. But they had mounted bicycles and ridden away, as though Billerby held no future for them. There was no sign of life in the one street and the two side streets of Billerby. Her footsteps disturbed various shut-up dogs, and in one house an aged person was coughing. That was the only house with a lighted window. Either the people of Billerby went to bed very early, or they all had television sets. There were, however, only a few aerials—as far as she could tell. The dusk and the gathering mist made it difficult to be sure.

However, there was the public call box, and when she shut herself into it the light went on like a public illumination. The light showed her that her purse held four pennies, one halfpenny and a five-pound note. Excellent! The pennies would pay the local call to some near-by garage; the note would look after the rest. Unfortunately, the call box had no Trades Directory book. She went and banged on the post office door. Nothing resulted except more barks and the wailing of an infant. She went back to the call box, and began to read through the ordinary directory, beginning with an Abacus Laundry. The public illumination did not seem so brilliant now, the print was small. She read from Abacus to Alsop, Mrs. Yolande, and found no garage. Perseverance had never been Belinda's forte. Moreover, honour was satisfied, and when reduced by famine it is not disgraceful to yield. She took off the receiver. She dialled O. She gave the Snewdon number.

'Put ninepence in the box, please.'

'I can't. I've only got fourpence; the rest must be collect.'

'We don't usually . . .'

'I'm not usual. I'm desperate.'

The operator laughed and put her through.

'This is Snewdon Beeleigh two two-seven.'

'Mother.'

'This is Snewdon Beeleigh two two-seven.'

'Mother.'

'This is Snewdon Beeleigh two two-seven. Can't you hear me?'

'Mother!'

'This is Snewdon . . .'

'Press button A, caller,' said the operator.

Belinda pressed button A and said icily, 'Mother?'

'Belinda! Oh, thank heavens! Where are you, what happened to you? I've been in such a state—we both have. Leo! Leo! She's found!' The shriek seemed to be in the very call box.

'When did you get home?'

'When did we get home? I haven't the slightest idea. I was far too worried to notice when we got home. What I've been through! We waited and waited. At last I said to Leo, "I'll stay here in case she comes back, and you go and find a man to drive us." What I felt—every minute like an hour—and the flies! . . . By the way, I saw a nightjar.'

'A nightjar? Are you sure it wasn't a hawk?'

'My dear child, I wasn't so frantic about you that I didn't know the difference between a hawk and a nightjar. Well, then I began to think Leo was swallowed up, too. I'd told him exactly how to get to Gamble's farm, but for all that, he went wrong and wandered all over the place, till at last he saw a spire, and it turned out to be my dear old Archdeacon Brownlow, and he came at once and rescued us. And ever since then, we've been ringing up the police, and the hospital, and the A.A. and Leo has been driving everywhere we could think of to look for you, he's only just come in. Yes, Leo, she's perfectly all right, I'm talking to her. And I don't wish to judge you, Belinda, till I've heard what you've got to say for yourself, but this I must say—it was the most horrible picnic of my life and I never want to live through another. Now I suppose I shall have to ring up the police and say it was all a false alarm. How I hate grovelling to officials!'

'While you're about it, you might ring up the A.A. too —about the car.'

'The car? . . . Oh, my God!'

'And tell them to fetch it away tomorrow.'.

'Fetch it? What's happened to it?'

'I ran out of petrol.'

'Well, why can't you have some put in, and bring it back? I can't do without it, I shall need it tomorrow, for I must take the Mothers' Union banner to Woffam to be invisibly darned and I want to take some gooseberries over to the Archdeacon, who was so very kind—and tactful. Not a single question, not one word of surprise. Just driving us home in such a soothing, understanding way. Leo thought him——'

Belinda slammed down the receiver. A minute later, the operator rang up Snewdon Beeleigh two two-seven to say there would be a collect charge of one and twopence on the call from Billerby. This time the telephone was answered by Leo.

The call-box door was not constructed to slam. Belinda closed it. The public illumination went out, and there was Billerby, unchanged. She had never lost her temper with so little satisfaction. She could not even enjoy her usual sensation of turning cold, for she was cold already. 'Well, at any rate, I've done my duty by them,' she said to herself. 'They know I'm alive and that the car isn't a wreck. And I've got five pounds and a halfpenny. With five pounds and a halfpenny I can at least buy one night to myself.'

But where was it to be bought, that idyllic night in a lumpy rural bed? For now it was ten o'clock, an hour at which people become disinclined to make up beds for strangers who arrive on foot and without luggage. Farther down the street, a light went on in an upper window —some carefree person going to bed as usual. She knocked on the door. The lighted window opened; an old man looked out.

'Who's there?'

'My car's broken down. Where can I find a bed for the night?'

'I don't know about that. It's a bit late to come asking for beds.' He looked up and down the street. 'Where's your car? I don't see no car.'

'On Frogwick Level. By the decoy.'

'That's a pity. If it had broken down nearer, you could have slept in it. Won't do it no good, either, standing out all night in the mermaid. These mermaids, they come from the sea, you see, so they're salt. That'll rust a car in no time.'

Like Mother, he thought of the car's welfare first. But he called the sea mist a mermaid: there must be some good in him.

'I don't want to stand out in it all night, either.'

'No, course you don't. So the best thing you can do, Missy, is to wait round about till the bus comes back.'

'The bus?'

'Bringing them back from the concert, you see. The concert at Shopdon, with the Comic. Everyone's gone to it. That's why there won't be no one here you could ask till they come back.'

'I see. Do you think . . .'

'They might and they mightn't. Of course, it will be a bit late by then.' He remained looking down, she remained looking up. Then he shook his head and closed the window. A moment later, the light went out. He must be undressing in the dark, as a safeguard.

Hunger and cold and discouragement narrowed her field of vision; she could see nothing to do but to walk up and down till the bus came back, and then plead with its passengers for a night's lodging. They would be full of merriment, flown with the Comic. . . . It wouldn't be very pleasant. She didn't look forward to it. Besides, they would be a crowd. It is vain to appeal to simple-hearted people when they are a crowd: embarrassment stiffens them, they shun the limelight of a good deed. She walked up and down and tried not to think of food—for this made her mouth water, which is disgraceful. She lit a cigarette. It made her feel sick. She threw it away.

It was a pity she couldn't throw herself away.

Opposite the shop that sold baby clothes was a Wesleyan chapel. It stood back from the road and produced an echo. Every time she passed by it she heard her footsteps sounding more dispirited. In front of the chapel was a railed yard, with some headstones and two table tombs. One can sit on a table tomb. She tried the gate. It was locked. Though she could have climbed the railings easily enough, she did not, but continued to walk up and down.

She might just as well throw herself away: she had always hated hoarding. Tomorrow it would all begin again—Mother's incessant shamming, rows and reconciliations with Leo. 'Darling, how could you behave like this?' 'Belinda, I despair of making you out.' 'It's not like you to be so callous.' 'Very well, very well! I am sorry I've been such a brute as to love you.' Or else they would combine to love her with all her faults. 'Darling, as you are back, I wonder if you could sometimes remember to turn off the hot tap properly.' But to throw oneself away—unless, like Uncle Henry, one is sensible and always goes about with a gun—one must do it off something or under something. The Wesleyan chapel was such a puny building that even if she were to scale it and throw herself off its pediment, she would be unlikely to do more than break her leg. And though there had once been a branch line to Frogwick, British Railways had closed it on the ground that it wasn't made use of. She could have made use of it. One would squirm through the wire fence, lie down on the track, hear the reliable iron approach, feel the rails tremble . . . 'and the light by which she had read the book filled with troubles, falsehoods, sorrow and evil . . .'

But she was in Billerby, not Moscow. On the outskirts of Billerby, and just about to turn round and walk back towards the Wesleyan chapel, the post office, the vacant shop that was for sale, the aged person coughing. An aged person coughing. That, too, lay ahead of her.

A light sprang up on the dark. A dazzle of headlights rushed towards her, creating vast shapes of roadside elms and overthrowing them, devouring night, perspective, space. She fluttered into its path like a moth. The Bristol swerved, braked, swung round on a skid, came to a stop across the road. Leo ran to where she stood motionless, with her mouth open.

'Damn you, Belinda, you fool!'

'Why are you here? Why can't I have a moment's peace? Go away!'

'I'd like to wring your neck.'

'Wring it then! Do something positive for a change.'

'Tripping out into the road like that. Do you realize I nearly killed you?'

'I wish you had! I wish you had!'

They clung together and shouted recriminations in each other's face. The driver of an approaching bus slowed down, and sounded his horn. As they ignored it, he stopped.

'Of course I did it deliberately. I drove away, and I stayed away, because I was tired of being talked at, and made a butt of—and bored, bored, bored! Do you think I've got no sensibilities?'

'Sensibilities? About as much as a rhinoceros.'

'Rhinoceros yourself!'

One by one, the party from the concert climbed out of the bus and walked cautiously towards this mysterious extra number.

'A pretty pair of fools you looked, sitting there with the picnic basket! And there you sat . . . and there you sat . . . .'

She broke into hysterical laughter. Leo cuffed her.

'Here! I say, young man . . . .'

They turned and saw the party from the concert gathering round them.

'Oh, damn these people!'

They ran to the car, leaped in, drove away. Several quick-witted voices exclaimed, 'Take the number! Take the number!' But the car went so fast, there wasn't time.

# HAPPINESS

'THE bathroom's the awkwardest feature,' said Mr. Naylor, of Elwes & Sons, house agents, 'being situated on the ground floor. People don't like ground-floor bathrooms. You might say, they just won't hear of them.'

'No, I suppose not. Yet . . .' Lavinia Benton broke off.

'I know what you were going to say, Mrs. Benton. You were going to say, Why not convert the dressing room upstairs, leaving the bathroom for what one might call a playroom, or a children's lounge, or a study, if there happened to be no family. Once we'd got the bath out, it could be called ideal for that, being so inordinately large for a bathroom. But then the pipes would have to be carried upstairs. Think of the plumbing, Mrs. Benton! Prohibitive! No buyer would contemplate it, not for this class of residence—it isn't as if this were one of those old oak jobs. And I understand you don't want to let the estate in for any extra expense. So there we are, I'm afraid. Back where we started from!'

Mr. Naylor had, in fact, scotched a snake that wasn't there. Lavinia's 'Yet' had been provoked by the reflection that an increasingly large acreage of southern England was occupied between 7.30 and 8.30 a.m. by people resignedly bathing on ground level. Not so resignedly, either, since there are always buyers for bungalows. Both Mr. Petherick, of Petherick, Petherick & Sampson, and Mr. Cox, of Ransom & Titters, had already explained that Aller

Lodge, the late Miss Esther Jeudwine's brick-built, two-storey residence in sound repair, would have been easy enough to sell if only it had been a bungalow. All a matter of social psychology, thought Lavinia who, as a columnist on superior Women's Pages, was accustomed to making something out of not much; a mass apprehension of being surprised with no clothes on, which if not primitive, since primitive man had other and more pressing things to be surprised by, must certainly go a long way back, being later reinforced by class distinction—the wealthy are draped, the poor go bare—and Christianity's insistence on modesty; for though a fakir can be venerable in a light handful of marigolds, an archdeacon can scarcely leave off his gaiters. In short, the discomposure of being surprised with no clothes on is, like the pleasurability of possessing a virgin, one of the things long taken for granted—and really even more of an *idée reçue,* being subscribed to by both sexes alike. Yet here was this mass apprehension, fortified by tradition, smoothed by acceptance, part of the British way of life, suddenly ceasing to function when brought into bungalows, where the hazards that might justify it—housebreakers, mad dogs, cars out of control, voyeurs, private detectives, almost anything, in fact, except the atom bomb—would be much more on the cards. But one must remember that bathrooms being so recent an introduction, public opinion could not have made up its mind about them yet, and was bound to be rather hypothetical.

Lavinia became aware that Mr. Naylor was observing her with sympathy, but at the same time giving little coughs. Of course. The poor man wanted to go.

'Well, goodbye, Mr. Naylor. And thank you for being

so helpful. I'm afraid it's a bad lookout, but I'm sure you'll do your best.'

'I'll do my best,' he said, and his voice, being more sincere than hers, sounded less sanguine.

She was almost sorry to see him go, he was so much the nicest of them, and the only one to show the slightest comprehension of the fix she was in. Nothing could have been more straightforward than Cousin Esther's will. Her legacies were proportionate to her estate and left a proper margin for expenses. A short list of remembrance gifts—and she had kept it up to date—was pinned to the will itself. She wished for a funeral service without hymns. She willed her house and personal property, other than the items specified in the attached list, to be sold and the proceeds to form a trust fund for the education of her great-great-nieces, Emily and Jemima Jeudwine, any residue to be divided between them when they reached the age of twenty-one (they were twins); and she appointed Hugh Dickenson Jeudwine and Lavinia Benton as her executors. Unfortunately, Hugh had died of his injuries a few hours after the car crash in which his great-aunt had been killed, and the house which was to provide the mainstay of the trust for Hugh's three-year-old daughters was proving unsellable.

During the four months of her executorship Lavinia's snatched visits to Aller Lodge, at first so nostalgic and so executive, had become heartless and vacant. The two servants, a married couple named Mullins, had received their legacies and gone off to let lodgings in Felixstowe; the cat, Dollop, had gone with them. The gifts had been dispatched; the best of the furniture, china and books had gone to the auction rooms in the county town, the silver, the Dutch flower paintings and the collection of clocks to Sotheby's. Remarking that this was no era for fish kettles (thereby providing Lavinia with the germ of half a column about the effects of broadcasting in Mandarin English to English listeners who with their native genius for phrase-making would seize on some devitalized term like 'era' and burnish it into a new arrestingness), the local second-hand dealer had removed several miscellaneous vanloads. What remained was just enough to emphasize that the house needed considerable repair and total redecoration.

Being so empty, it seemed brimful of the noise of the traffic speeding past its ironwork railings and the laurel hedge that protected the long narrow garden. 'All those laurels, too,' Mr. Petherick had commented. 'Who's going to keep up laurels nowadays? Laurels are O-U-T Out!'

Yet on Lavinia's visits to Cousin Esther she had never noticed the noise of traffic. During the day, they had so much to say to each other; and Lavinia's bedroom was at the back, looking straight into the pear tree.

'Well, child, here we are, all ready for a nice long talk. Sit down, dear. Have you brought any parlour work?'

'My petit point.'

'Let me look at it. H'm. Not too bad, not too bad. Is this the same panel you brought last time? Oh, well, no doubt you've got other things to do in London. Now tell me the latest nonsense.'

'Red flannel nightdresses, with long sleeves, high necks and crochet lace edgings.'

'We had featherstitching. Far more practical, and didn't rag out in the wash.' If Lavinia had cited starched ruffs, ankle-length pantalettes or tiffany aprons as being the latest nonsenses it would turn out that Cousin Esther had worn them, with improvements. 'Will you have a cigar?'

'Not till after dinner, thank you.'

The cigars had begun when Lavinia decided to leave her husband and earn her own living, and they were Cousin Esther's idea. 'You aren't shocked, are you, at my taking a job?' Lavinia had asked. Since childhood, Cousin Esther's approval had been her fortress. And Cousin Esther had said, 'Shocked, dear? Why should I be? Now you can give up those trivial little cigarettes and smoke cigars. I've always liked George Sand. Charming woman, and so capable. But keep to cigars, duckie; you aren't made for de Mussets.'

Now there was only the noise of traffic, for Cousin Esther was in her grave, and the Boulle clock and the clock that played *Partant pour la Syrie* were ticking at Sotheby's; and the house—the only house where Lavinia smoked cigars—was for sale and no one would buy it.

A section of the noise stopped at the gate. The doorbell rang. A possible buyer? But it was Mr. Naylor back again, back with something in his jaws: his expression plainly said so.

'Mrs. Benton, I've had an idea. I was thinking about those laurels as I drove along, what a job it would be to keep them trimmed. "Another handicap" I said to myself. Handicap! Why, it's the main feature, though I didn't realize it until one of our own "FOR SALE" boards caught my eye, just outside Beck St. Mary's, "AMPLE FRONTAGE" Ample frontage! If ever there was ample frontage, we've got it here. So I turned straight round and came back. And here I am.'

'In time for a cup of tea,' she said. 'I'm just making my-self one. Do sit down. I won't be a moment.'

She knew and she did not know. What she unequivo-cally knew was that unless she kept a firm hand on herself, she was going to be silly.

When she carried in the tray, the French windows had been opened and Mr. Naylor was walking up the garden, looking pleased as Adam. He came in, rubbing his hands, flowing with kindheartedness.

'Yes, Mrs. Benton, it's perfect; couldn't be better. You can forget about that bathroom now. All we've got to do is to apply for a building permit. And you'll get it, never fear. All this end of Long Monkton is scheduled for de-velopment, now that we're getting the bypass. Yes, you'll soon be out of your troubles. I've been pacing it. There's ample room for two.'

'Two?' she said, holding on to the teapot.

'Two bungalows,' said Mr. Naylor, as though he were promising oranges to a child—to a Victorian child in a pinafore, to whom oranges meant oranges. Two bunga-lows. Two families bathing in confidence in Cousin Esther's garden.

'Two bungalows?'

'With garages. Up as soon as winking,' said Mr. Naylor. 'And double the money you were hoping to get for the place as it is.'

Double the money. And if not double the thankfulness of Hugh's widow—who whatever she might be about to receive would retain a bleak unthankfulness—a possible ten-per-cent abatement in her conviction that because poor Hughie wasn't there to stand up for his children Lavinia would sell the house to the first comer who offered sixpence for it.

'Which I'm not likely to get, you think?'

'To be honest with you, which would always be my wish, not in a month of Sundays.'

A flimsy hope brushed her.

'Unfortunately, I don't think I could afford to build.'

'Build? Heaven forbid! Why, they'd ruin you. No, no, what you've got to do is to sell as building land. Once you've got the permit through, it'll sell before we can say "knife".'

Two rather tipsy butterflies that had been feasting in the buddleia chased each other in through the French window and chased each other out again. Mr. Naylor and me saying 'knife', she thought.

'Two bungalows,' she repeated.

'Or it might be three,' said Mr. Naylor, wooing her with three oranges, since only a couple appeared to have fallen rather flat with this lady. 'Yes, that's quite a possibility. For the right sort of buyer, someone with enterprise and enough labour, would think nothing of demolishing the house and putting the third bungalow here, where we are sitting. He could use a lot of the bricks; the lead on the roof alone would be worth a fortune. You could ask according, and get it.'

'But the pear tree!'

'True, that's an item. These old trees, their roots get everywhere. But half an hour with a bulldozer—you'd be surprised. Isn't that the front door?'

The lady dotted with mink carried an order to view from Ransom & Titters. 'Sweet old place, isn't it?' she remarked. 'Georgian all over. I never tire of Georgian. It's got so much character.'

'I'm afraid this is Victorian.'

'Oh! Then why does it look so Georgian? I suppose it was an imitation.'

She was so plainly no buyer that Lavinia did not even feel the adulterous embarrassment of being interrupted while drinking tea with one house agent by the client of another. Mr. Naylor was not embarrassed, either. Combining tact with business, he returned to the garden and paced it more scrupulously. The dotted lady was scrupulous, too. Before she left, she had gone into every room, opened every closet, asked every question, saying in the tone of one worn out by bestowing benefits, 'Really? Quite quaint!'

Mr. Naylor said chivalrously that with ladies of that kind it was hard to tell. Something might come of her.

'Horrible woman!' said Lavinia. By contrast, Mr. Naylor seemed such a bosom friend that she allowed her voice to express some of the dejection she felt. If he felt that dejection was a poor response to the happy issue he had opened before her, he did not show it. He remembered something he must be getting along to, thanked her for the tea, said he would leave her to think it over. In the morning, all she would have to do would be to give him a tinkle. He would bring the application forms and see to the rest.

Still fending it off, she went through the house, opening doors and windows. The lady who adored Georgian had a Georgian insensibility to stinks, and her perfume resounded like a cornet. There was the bedroom, the defrauded bedroom in which Cousin Esther had not died. Everything had gone wrong at the last; the house had been robbed of its due.

'I might as well say Done,' she said to herself, at last. 'Say Done, and say Goodbye.'

Goodbye is a thing best said out-of-doors. She went out,

and walked up and down the long flower border, being careful not to glance towards the house, to which the opened windows gave a curious air of animation, of a party being held. She looked at the flowers; she noticed the strong growth of late summer weeds. The jobbing gardener she had hired to give the place a tidy-up was not thorough like Mullins. Never mind, never mind! The flowers did not seem to mind, either; the zinnias, the hollyhocks, the velvety dahlias looked exceptionally sumptuous and thriving. One must admit that flowers prefer the company of weeds to the company of a weeder. Their loyalty is to the vegetable kingdom; they are delighted to get away from the fostering, censuring, interfering guardianship of man. All at once, a dahlia shed its petals. She realized that for the last ten minutes she had not been looking at the flowers; she had not even been conscious of them, she had been exploiting them, spinning a true observation into another whimsical paragraph. Never mind, never mind! Come to that, Mullins would have sent them to the flower show. No wonder they felt more at home with their weeds.

Slowly, with hanging head, she walked across the lawn towards the pear tree. It was an old tree. It was said to have been there before Aller Lodge was built; it was already tall and thick-limbed when Cousin Esther arrived, and none could name it. Its fruit, a dark obsidian green, smooth-rinded, narrow, almost cylindrical, ripened very late and kept throughout the winter. Being so old, the pear tree was also rather fitful and cranky. In the spring of last year it had bloomed so abundantly, so triumphantly, that Cousin Esther had telegraphed to her to come and see it. This year, so Mullins reported when she came for the funeral, there had been a very poor show of bloom and no bees. She laid her hand on its rough bark. 'I have sold you,' she said. At the sound of her words, tears of shame started painfully from her eyes. Shaking her head to free her cheeks of them, she looked up and saw something white. It was a cluster of pear blossoms, newly, perfectly unfolded.

It was startling—she need not let it be more. It was the whim of an old tree, and in fact she had seen other such blossomings in other Augusts. To hear a cuckoo would have been much more remarkable. The blossoms' extreme whiteness enforced the sudden presence of dusk. She must go in and shut those windows before dewfall. She sat down on the plank bench that encircled the trunk of the tree. Suppose she bought the house? She could not afford to; she didn't really want to. Suppose she bought the house? Not from sentiment, not from piety, not from resentment of bungalows, but for her own pleasure. She would keep her old bedroom, of course, smelling the pear blossom in the early morning, sharing bees with it, hearing a pear fall, and another pear fall, as she lay under the eiderdown on the first frosty night, and thinking how, first thing in the morning, she would go down and hunt for them in the long grass. After a time—there need be no hurry about it—Cousin Esther's bedroom would become her spare room, and Emily and Jemima, who by then would be old enough to go visiting without their mother, would sleep there, feeling grand in a grown-up bed, as she had felt, and supported by a night light, as she had been. The traffic would not disturb them—besides, by then the bypass would have taken most of it away; the laurel hedge would be a boundary again. She would repaint the white seat. At night she would go round, locking up the house, turning the familiar, heavy, infallible keys, and afterwards she would lie in the ground-floor bathroom, hearing the owls hooting, and looking at the map of Europe, which fortunately even the reluctant fish-kettle remover had refused to take away. If she bought the house, she would buy other things, too. She would buy an inkpot, a penholder, a packet of steel nibs—and never touch her typewriter again. There should be no more clever slavery. To be on the safe side, she would not even keep a diary, and 'LAVINIA BENTON' would vanish from the printed page until it made its curt farewell appearance in the deaths column. Till then, she would be Mrs. Benton, an ageing English lady with a winter hat and a summer hat, who sometimes went to church, who sometimes smoked a cigar after dinner, who sat reading by candlelight because it is more restful for the eyes, or for some such decorous reason. The candlelight would be known because its glow would be seen through the gap in the curtains; no one would know the exquisite pleasure she would find in the smell of sweet wax, lingering on into the next morning. No one would know, since she would not speak of it.

As though her moderate intention of churchgoing had encouraged the church clock, it now chimed a quarter. Looking at her watch, she found it was too dark to read its face. Car lights were stabbing through the laurel hedge. Gently, she got up; gently, she laid her lips to the rough bark of the tree, and kissed it a gentle farewell. It had put out its cluster of blossom—a pure statement of spring, since nothing would come of it. It had given her an hour of happiness.

# A LOVE MATCH

It was Mr. Pilkington who brought the Tizards to Hallowby. He met them, a quiet couple, at Carnac, where he had gone for a schoolmasterly Easter holiday to look at the monoliths. After two or three meetings at a café, they invited him to their rented chalet. It was a cold, wet afternoon and a fire of pine cones crackled on the hearth. 'We collect them on our walks,' said Miss Tizard. 'It's an economy. And it gives us an object.' The words, and the formal composure of her manner, made her seem like a Frenchwoman. Afterwards, he learned that the Tizards were a Channel Island family and had spent their childhood in Jersey. The ancestry that surfaced in Miss Tizard's brisk gait and erect carriage, brown skin and compact sentences, did not show in her brother. His fair hair, his red face, his indecisive remarks, his diffident movements—as though with the rest of his body he were apologizing for his stiff leg—were entirely English. He ought not, thought Mr. Pilkington, to be hanging about in France. He'd done more than enough for France already. For this was in 1923 and Mr. Pilkington, with every intention of preserving a historian's impartiality, was nevertheless infected by the current mood of disliking the French.

The weather continued cold and wet; there was a sameness about the granite avenues. Mr. Pilkington's mind became increasingly engaged with the possibility, the desirability, the positive duty of saving that nice fellow

Tizard from wasting his days in exile. He plied him with hints, with suggestions, with tactful inquiries. Beyond discovering that money was not the obstacle to return, he got no further. Tizard, poor fellow, must be under his sister's thumb. Yet it was from the sister that he got his first plain answer. 'Justin would mope if he had nothing to do.' Mr. Pilkington stopped himself from commenting on the collection of pine cones as an adequate lifework. As though she had read his thought, she went on, 'There is a difference between idling in a foreign country and being an idler in your own.' At that moment Tizard limped into the room with crayfish bristling from his shopping basket. 'It's begun,' he said ruefully. '*La Jeune France* has arrived. I've just seen two young men in pink trousers with daisy chains round their necks, riding through the town on donkeys.' Mr. Pilkington asked if this was a circus. Miss Tizard explained that it was the new generation, and would make Carnac a bedlam till the summer's end. 'Of course, there's a certain amount of that sort of thing in England, too,' observed Mr. Pilkington. 'But only in the South. It doesn't trouble us at Hallowby.' As he spoke, he was conscious of playing a good card; then the immensity of the trump he held broke upon him. He was too excited to speak. Inviting them to dine at his hotel on the following night, he went away.

By next evening, more of *La Jeune France* had arrived, and was mustered outside the hotel extemporizing a bull-fight ballet in honour of St. Cornély, patron saint of cattle and of the parish church. Watching Tizard's look of stoically endured embarrassment Mr. Pilkington announced that he had had a blow; the man who had almost promised to become curator of the Beelby Military

Museum had written to say he couldn't take up the post. 'He didn't say why. But I know why. Hallowby is too quiet for him.'

'But I thought Hallowby had blast furnaces and strikes and all that sort of thing,' said Tizard.

'That is Hallowby juxta Mare,' replied Mr. Pilkington. 'We are Old Hallowby. Very quiet; quite old, too. The school was founded in 1623. We shall be having our modest tercentenary this summer. That is why I am so put out by Dalsover's not taking up the curatorship. I hoped to have the museum all in order. It would have been something to visit, if it rains during the Celebrations.' He allowed a pause.

Tizard, staring at the toothpicks, inquired, 'Is it a wet climate?'

But Mr. Pilkington was the headmaster of a minor public school, a position of command. As if the pause had not taken place, raising his voice above the bullfight he told how fifty years earlier Davenport Beelby, a rich man's sickly son, during a lesson on the Battle of Minden awoke to military glory and began to collect regimental buttons. Buttons, badges, pikes, muskets and bayonets, shakos and helmets, despatches, newspaper cuttings, stones from European battlefields, sand from desert campaigns—his foolish collection grew into the lifework of a devoted eccentric and, as such collections sometimes do, became valuable and authoritative, though never properly catalogued. Two years ago he had died, bequeathing the collection to his old school, with a fund sufficient for upkeep and the salary of a curator.

'I wish you'd consider coming as our curator,' said Mr. Pilkington. 'I'm sure you would find it congenial. Beelby wanted an Army man. Three mornings a week would be quite enough.'

Tizard shifted his gaze from the toothpicks to the mustard jar. 'I am not an Army man,' he said. 'I just fought. Not the same thing, you know.'

Miss Tizard exclaimed, 'No! Not at all,' and changed the subject.

But later that evening she said to her brother, 'Once we were there, we shouldn't see much of him. It's a possibility.'

'Do you want to go home, Celia?'

'I think it's time we did. We were both of us born for a sober, conventional, taxpaying life, and if——'

'*Voici Noël!*' sang the passing voices. '*Voici Noël! Voici Noël, petits enfants!*'

She composed her twitching hands and folded them on her lap. 'We were young rowdies once,' he said placatingly.

A fortnight later, they were Mr. Pilkington's guests at Hallowby. A list of empty houses had been compiled by Miss Robson, the secretary. All were variously suitable; each in turn was inspected by Miss Tizard and rejected. Mr. Pilkington felt piqued that his offer of a post should dance attendance on the aspect of a larder or the presence of decorative tiles. Miss Tizard was a disappointment to him; he had relied on her support. Now it was the half-hearted Tizard who seemed inclined to root, while she flitted from one eligible residence to another, appearing, as he remarked to the secretary, to expect impossibilities. Yet when she settled as categorically as a queen bee the house she chose had really nothing to be said for it. A square, squat mid-Victorian box, Newton Lodge was one of the ugliest houses in Hallowby; though a high surrounding wall with a green door in it hid the totality of its ugliness from passers-by, its hulking chimneys proclaimed what was below. It was not even well situated. It stood in a deteriorating part of the town, and was at some distance from the school buildings and the former gymnasium—Victorian also—which had been assigned to the Beelby Collection. But the house having been chosen, the curatorship was bestowed and the move made. Justin Tizard, rescued from wasting his days in exile—though too late for the tercentenary celebrations—began his duties as curator by destroying a quantity of cobwebs and sending for a window-cleaner.

All through the summer holidays he worked on, sorting things into heaps, subdividing the heaps into lesser heaps. Beelby's executors must have given carte-blanche to the packers, who had acted on the principle of rilling up with anything that came handy, and the unpackers had done little more than tumble things out and scatter them with notices saying 'DO NOT DISTURB'. The largest heap consisted of objects he could not account for, but unaccountably it lessened, till the day came when he could look round on tidiness. Ambition seized him. Tidiness is not enough; no one looks twice at tidiness. There must also be parade and ostentation. He bought stands, display cases, dummies for the best uniforms. Noticing a decayed wooden horse in the saddler's shop, he bought that, too; trapped, with its worser side to the wall and with a cavalry dummy astride, it made a splendid appearance. He combed plumes, shook out bearskins, polished holsters and gunstocks, oiled the demi-culverin, sieved the desert sand. At this stage, his sister came and polished with him, mended, refurbished, sewed on loose buttons. Of the two, she had more feeling for the exhibits themselves, for the discolouring glory and bloodshed they represented. It was the housewife's side that appealed to him. Sometimes, hearing him break into the whistle of a contented mind, she would look up from her work and stare at him with the unbelief of thankfulness.

Early in the autumn term, Mr. Pilkington made time to visit the museum. He did not expect much and came prepared with speeches of congratulation and encouragement. They died on his lips when he saw the transformation. Instead, he asked how much the display cases had cost, and the dummies, and the horse, and how much of the upkeep fund remained after all this expenditure. He could not find fault; there was no reason to do so. He was pleased to see Tizard so well established as master in his own house. Perhaps he was also pleased that there was no reason to find fault. Though outwardly unchanged, the Tizard of Carnac appeared to have been charged with new contents—with something obstinately reckless beneath the easy-going manner, with watchfulness beneath the diffidence. But this, reflected Mr. Pilkington, might well be accounted for by the startling innovations in the museum. He stayed longer than he meant, and only after leaving remembered that he had omitted to say how glad he was that Tizard had accepted the curatorship. This must be put right; he did not want to discourage the young man who had worked so hard and so efficiently, and also he must get into the way of remembering that Tizard was in fact a young man—under thirty. Somehow, one did not think of him as a young man.

*

Justin Tizard, newly a captain in an infantry regiment, came on leave after the battle of the Somme. His sister met the train at Victoria. There were some pigeons strutting on the platform and he was watching them when a strange woman in black came up to him, touched his shoulder, and said, 'Justin!' It was as though Celia were claiming a piece of lost luggage, he thought. She had a taxi waiting, and they drove to her flat. She asked about his health, about his journey; then she congratulated him on his captaincy. 'Practical reasons,' he said. 'My habit of not getting killed. They were bound to notice it sooner or later.' After this, they fell silent. He looked out of the window at the streets so clean and the people so busy with their own affairs. 'That's a new Bovril poster, isn't it?' he inquired. Her answer was so slow in coming that he didn't really take in whether it was yes or no.

Her flat was new, anyway. She had only been in it since their mother's remarriage. It was up a great many flights of stairs, and she spoke of moving to somewhere with a lift, now that Tim's legacy had made a rich woman of her. The room smelled of polish and flowers. There was a light-coloured rug on the floor and above this was the blackness of Celia's skirts. She was wearing black for her fiancé. The news of his death had come to her in this same room, while she was still sorting books and hanging pictures. Looking round the room, still not looking at Celia, he saw Tim's photograph on her desk. She saw his glance, and hers followed it. 'Poor Tim!' they said, both speaking at once, the timbre of their voices relating them. 'They say he was killed instantaneously,' she went on. 'I hope it's true—though I suppose they always say that.'

'I'm sure it is,' he replied. He knew that Tim had been

blown to pieces. Compassion made it possible to look at her. Dressed in black, possessing these new surroundings, she seemed mature and dignified beyond her actual three years' seniority. For the first time in his life he saw her not as a sister but as an individual. But he could not see her steadily for long. There was a blur on his sight, a broth of mud and flame and frantic unknown faces and writhing entrails. When she showed him to his bedroom she stepped over mud that heaved with the bodies of men submerged in it. She had drawn the curtains. There was a bed with sheets turned back, and a bedside lamp shed a serene, un-blinking light on the pillows. 'Bed!' he exclaimed, and heard the spontaneity die in his voice. 'Wonderful to see a bed!'

'And this is the bathroom. I've got everything planned. First of all, you must have a bath, lie and soak in it. And then put on these pyjamas and the dressing gown, and we will have supper.'

Left to himself, he was violently sick. Shaking with fatigue, he sat in a hot scented bath and cleaned his knees with scrupulous care, like a child. Outside was the noise of London.

The pyjamas were silk, the dressing gown was quilted and wrapped him round like a caress. In the sitting room was Celia, still a stranger, though now a stranger without a hat. There was a table sparkling with silver and crystal, smoked salmon, a bottle of champagne, It was all as she had planned it for Tim—Oh, poor Celia!

They discussed their mother's remarriage. It had been decided on with great suddenness, and appeared inexplic-able. Though they refrained from saying much, their comments implied that her only reason for marrying a meat king from the Argentine was to get away from England and the war. 'There he was, at eleven in the morning, with a carnation—a foot shorter than she,' said Celia, describing the return from the registry office.

'In that case, he must be four foot three.'

'He is exactly four foot three. I stole up and measured him.'

Spoken in her imperturbable voice, this declaration struck him as immensely funny, as funny as a nursery joke. They laughed hilariously, and after this their evening went almost naturally.

Turning back after his unadorned, brotherly 'Good night, Celia,' he exclaimed, 'But where are you sleeping?'

'In here.' Before he could demur she went on, 'The sofa fits me. It would be far too short for you.'

He told her how balmily he had slept, one night behind the lines, with his head on a bag of nails.

'Exactly! That is why tonight you are going to sleep properly. In a bed.'

She heard him get into bed, heard the lamp switched off. Almost immediately she heard his breathing lengthen into slumber. Then, a few minutes later, he began to talk in his sleep.

Perhaps a scruple—the dishonourableness of being an eavesdropper, a Peeping Tom—perhaps mere craven terror, made her try not to listen. She began to read, and when she found that impossible she repeated poems she had learned at school, and when that failed she polished the silver cigarette box. But Justin's voice was raised, and the partition wall was thin, and the ghastly confidences went on and on. She could not escape them. She was dragged, a raw recruit. into battle.

In the morning she thought she would not be able to look him in the face. But he was cheerful, and so was she. She had got off from the canteen, she explained, while he was on leave; they had nothing to do but enjoy themselves. They decided to have some new experiences, so they went up the Monument. If he wants to throw himself off, she thought, I won't stop him. They looked down on London; on the curve of the Thames, the shipping, the busy lighters. They essayed how many City churches they could identify by their spires. They talked about Pepys. She would be surprised, Justin said, how many chaps carried a copy of the *Diary*, and she asked if bullets also glanced off Pepys carried in a breast pocket. So they made conversation quite successfully. And afterwards, when they had decided to go for a walk down Whitechapel High Street and lunch off winkles at a stall, many people glanced at them with kindness and sentimentality, and an old woman patted Celia's back, saying, 'God bless you, dearie! Isn't it lovely to have him home?'

Whitechapel was a good idea. The throng of people carried some of the weight of self-consciousness for them; the wind blowing up-river and the hooting of ships' sirens made them feel they were in some foreign port of call, taking a stroll till it was time to re-embark. He was less aware that she had grown strange to him, and she was momentarily able to forget the appalling stranger who had raved in her bed all night.

They dined at a restaurant, and went on to a music hall. That night he took longer to fall asleep. She had allowed herself a thread of hope, when he began to talk again. Three Justins competed, thrusting each other aside: a cold, attentive observer, a debased child, a devil bragging in hell.

At intervals they were banished by a recognizable Justin interminably muttering to himself, 'Here's a sword for Toad, here's a sword for Rat, here's a sword for Mole, here's a sword for Badger.' The reiteration from that bible of their childhood would stick on the word, 'Rat'. 'Got you!' And he was off again.

The next day they went to the Zoo. The Zoo was not so efficacious as Whitechapel. It was feeling the pinch, the animals looked shabby and dejected, many cages were empty. Two sleepless nights had made Celia's feet swell. It was pain to walk, pain to stand. She wondered how much longer she could keep it up, this 'God bless you, dearie' pretence of a lovely leave. The day accumulated its hours like a windlass. The load grew heavier; the windlass baulked under it, but wound on. He went to bed with the usual 'Good night, Celia'. As usual, she undressed and put on that derision of a nightdress, and wrapped herself in an eiderdown and lay down to wait under the smiling gaze of Tim's photograph. She felt herself growing icy cold, couldn't remember if she had wound her watch, couldn't remember what diversion she had planned for the morrow, was walking over Richmond Bridge in a snowstorm, when she noticed he had begun again. *She noticed*. It had come to that. Two nights of a vicarious endurance of what was being endured, had been endured, would continue to be endured by a cancelled generation, had so exhausted her that now she felt neither horror nor despair, merely a bitter acquiescence. Justin went on with his Hail Devil Rosary, and in France the guns went on and on, and the mud dried into dust and slumped back into mud again. People went down to Kent to listen to the noise of the guns: the people in Kent said that they had grown used to it, didn't hear it any longer. The icy cold sensation bored into her midriff, nailed her down in sleep.

Some outcry, some exclamation (she could not afterwards remember what it was), woke her. Before she knew what she was doing she was in the next room, trying to waken the man who lay so rigidly in her bed, who, if she could awaken him, would be Justin, her brother Justin. 'Oh, poor Justin, my poor Justin!' Throwing herself on the bed, she clasped him in her arms, lifted his head to lie against her breast, kissed his chattering lips. 'There, there!' She felt him relax, waken, drag her towards him. They rushed into the escape of love like winter-starved cattle rushing into a spring pasture.

When light came into the room, they drew a little apart and looked at each other.

'Now we've done it,' he said; and hearing the new note in his voice she replied, 'A good thing, don't you think?'

Their release left them no option. After a few hours they were not even astonished. They were mated for life, that was all—for a matter of days, so they made the most of it. At the end of his leave they parted in exaltation, he convinced that he was going off to be killed, she that she would bear his child, to which she would devote the remainder of her existence.

A little later she knew she was not pregnant.

Early in the new year Justin, still panoplied in this legendary and by now rather ludicrous charmed life, was made a major. In April, he was wounded in the leg. 'Nothing to worry about,' he wrote; 'just a few splinters. I am in bed, as peaceful as a pincushion.' Later, she heard that he had been moved to a hospital on the outskirts of

London. One of the splinters had escaped notice, and gas gangrene had developed in the wound.

I shall be a peg leg, he thought. It's not decent for a peg leg to make love; even to his sister. He was ravaged with fret and behaving with perfect decorum when Celia was shown in—dressed all in leaf green, walking like an empress, smelling delicious. For a moment the leaf-green Celia was almost as much of a stranger as the Celia all in black had been. When she kissed him, he discovered that she was shaking from head to foot. 'There, there,' he said, patting her. Still holding his hand, she addressed herself to charming Nurse Painter. Nurse Painter was in favour of sisters. They weren't so much trouble, didn't upset a patient, as sweethearts or wives did—and you didn't have to be hanging round all the time, ready to shoo them off. When Celia came next day, Nurse Painter congratulated her on having done the Major no end of good. There had been a lot of pus; she liked to see a lot of pus.

They continued to give satisfaction; when Justin left hospital with a knee that would always be stiff and from time to time cause him pain, Nurse Painter's approval went with them. A sister was just what he wanted—there would be no silly excitement; and as Miss Tizard was a trifle older than the Major, there would be a restraining hand if called for. If Nurse Painter had known what lay beneath this satisfactory arrangement, it is probable that her approval would not have been seriously withdrawn. The war looked like going on for ever; the best you could hope for was a stalemate. Potatoes were unobtainable, honesty was no more, it was hate and muddle wherever you looked. If a gentleman and lady could pluck up heart enough to love and be happy—well, good luck to them!

Justin and Celia went to Oxfordshire, where they com-pared the dragonflies on the Windrush with the dragon-flies on the Evenlode. Later, they went to France.

*

Beauty cannot be suborned. Never again did Justin see Celia quivering with beauty as she had done on the day she came to him in hospital. But he went on thinking she had a charming face and the most entertaining eyebrows in the world. Loving each other criminally and sincerely, they took pains to live together happily and to safeguard their happiness from injuries of their own infliction or from outside. It would have been difficult for them to be any-thing but inconspicuous, or to be taken for anything but a brother and sister—the kind of brother and sister of whom one says, 'It will be rather hard for her when he marries. Their relationship, so conveniently obvious to the public eye, was equally convenient in private life, for it made them unusually intuitive about each other's feelings. Brought up to the same standard of behaviour, using the same vocabulary, they felt no need to impress each other and were not likely to be taken aback by each other's likes and dislikes. Even the fact of remembering the same foxed copy of *The Swiss Family Robinson* with the tear across the picture of the boa constrictor was a reassuring bond. During the first years in France they felt they would like to have a child—or for the sake of the other's happiness ought to have a child—and discussed the possibilities of a child put out to nurse, learning French as its native speech, and then being adopted as a postwar orphan, since it was now too late for it to be a war orphan. But however the child was dated, it would be almost certain to declare its inheritance of Grandfather Tizard's nose, and as a fruitful incest is thought even worse of than a barren one, they sensibly gave up the idea; though regretting it.

Oddly enough, after settling in Hallowby they regretted it no longer. They had a home in England, a standing and things to do. Justin had the Beelby Museum; Celia had a household. In Hallowby it was not possible to stroll out to a restaurant or to bring home puddings from the pastry cook, fillets of veal netted into bolsters by the butcher. Celia had to cook seriously, and soon found that if she was to cook meals worth eating she must go shopping too. This was just what was needed for their peace and quiet, since to be seen daily shopping saved a great deal of repetitious explanation that she and Justin could not afford to keep a servant in the house but must be content with Mrs. Mugthwaite coming in three afternoons a week, and a jobbing gardener on Fridays. True, it exposed her to a certain amount of condolence and amazement from the school wives, but as they, like Mrs. Mugthwaite, came only in the afternoons, she could bear with it. Soon they came more sparingly; for, as Justin pointed out, poverty is the sturdiest of all shelters, since people feel it to be rather sad and soon don't think about it, whereas her first intention of explaining that ever since her Aunt Dinah had wakened in the middle of the night to see an angered cook standing over her with a meat hatchet she had been nervous of servants sleeping under the same roof would only provoke gossip, surmise and insistent recommendations of cooks without passions. Justin was more long-sighted than Celia. She always knew what to do or say at the moment. He could look ahead, foresee dangers, and take steps to dodge them.

They did not see as much of Mr. Pilkington as they had apprehended, and members of the staff were in no hurry to take up with another of Pilkington's Pets. Celia grew alarmed; if you make no friends, you become odd. She decided that they must occasionally go to church, though not too often or too enthusiastically, as it would then become odd that they did not take the Sacrament. No doubt a great many vicious church attenders took the Sacrament, and the rubric only forbids it to 'open and notorious evil-livers', which they had every intention of not being; but she could see a scruple of honour at work in Justin, so she did not labour this argument. There was a nice, stuffy pitch-pine St. Cuthbert's near by, and at judicious intervals they went there for evensong—thereby renewing another bond of childhood: the pleasure of hurrying home on a cold evening to eat baked potatoes hot from the oven. How old Mr. Gillespie divined from Justin's church demeanour that he was a whist player was a mystery never solved. But he divined it. He had barely saved Celia's umbrella from being blown inside out, remarking, 'You're newcomers, aren't you? You don't know the east wind at this corner,' before he was saying to Justin, 'You don't play whist, by any chance?' But probably he would have asked this of anyone not demonstrably a raving maniac, for since Colin Colbeck's death he, Miss Colbeck and Canon Pendarves were desperate for a fourth player. Canon Pendarves gave dinner parties, with a little music afterwards. Celia, driven into performance and remembering how Becky Sharp had wooed Lady Steyne by singing the religious songs of Mozart, sat down at the piano and played 'The Carmen's Whistle', one of the few things she reliably knew by heart. This audacious antiquarianism delighted the Canon, who kept her at his side for the rest of the evening, relating how he had once tried to get up a performance of Tallis's forty-part motet.

The Tizards were no longer odd. Their new friends were all considerably older than they; the middle-aged had more conscience about the war and were readier to make friends with a disabled major and his devoted maiden sister. In time, members of the staff overlooked their prejudice against Pilkington Pets and found the Tizard couple agreeable, if slightly boring.

Returning from their sober junketings Justin and Celia, safe within their brick wall, cast off their weeds of middle age, laughed, chattered and kissed with an intensified delight in their scandalous immunity from blame. They were a model couple, the most respectable couple in Hallowby, treading hand in hand the thornless path to fogydom. They began to give small dinner parties themselves. They set up a pug and a white cat. During their fifth summer in Hallowby they gave an evening party in the Beelby Museum. This dashing event almost carried them too far. It was such a success that they were begged to make an annual thing of it; and Celia was so gay, and her dress so fashionable, that she was within an inch of being thought a dangerous woman. Another party being expected of them, another had to be given. But this was a very different set-out: a children-and-parents party with a puppet show, held in St. Cuthbert's Church Room, with Canon Pendarves speaking on behalf of the Save the Children Fund and a collection taken at the door. The collection was a master stroke. It put the Tizards back in their place as junior fogies—where Justin, for his part, was thankful to be. He had got there a trifle prematurely, perhaps, being in his mid-thirties, but it was where he intended to end his days.

He was fond of gardening, and had taken to gardening seriously, having an analysis made of the Newton Lodge soil—too acid, as he suspected—buying phosphates and potash and lime and kainite, treating different plots with different mixtures and noting the results in a book. He could not dig, but he limpingly mowed and rolled the lawn, trained climbing roses and staked delphiniums. Within the shelter of the wall, delphiniums did magnificently. Every year he added new varieties and when the original border could be lengthened no further a parallel bed was dug, with a grass walk in between. Every summer evening he walked there, watching the various blues file off, some to darkness, some to pallor, as the growing dusk took possession of them, while the white cat flitted about his steps like a moth. Because one must not be wholly selfish, from time to time he would invite a pair of chosen children to tea, cut each of them a long delphinium lance (cutting only those which were going over, however) and set them to play jousting matches on the lawn. Most of them did no more than thwack, but the two little Semples, the children of the school chaplain, fought with system, husbanding their strokes and aiming at each other's faces. Even when they had outgrown jousting they still came to Newton Lodge, hunting snails, borrowing books, helping him weigh out basic slag, addressing him as 'Justin'.

'Mary is just the age our child would have been,' remarked Celia after one of these visits. Seeing him start at the words, she went on, 'When you went back to be killed, and I was quite sure I would have a baby.'

'I wouldn't stand being called Justin—if she were.'

'You might have to. They're Bright Young Things from the cradle on, nowadays.'

By now the vogue for being a Bright Young Thing had reached even to Hallowby, its ankles growing rather muddied and muscular on the way. It was not like Celia to prefer an inferior article, and Justin wondered to see her tolerance of this anglicization of the *Jeune France* when the original movement had so exasperated her. He hoped she wasn't mellowing; mellowness is not the food of love. A quite contrary process, however, was at work in Celia. At Carnac, even when accepting Pilkington as a way out of it, the exaltation of living in defiance of social prohibitions and the absorbing manœuvres of seeming to live in compliance with them had been stimulus enough; she had had no mercy for less serious rebels. But during the last few years the sense of sinking month by month into the acquiescence of Hallowby, eating its wholesome lotus like cabbage, conforming with the inattentiveness of habit— and aware that if she overlooked a conformity the omission would be redressed by the general conviction that Justin Tizard, though in no way exciting, was always so nice and had a sister who devoted her life to him, so nice for them both, etc. etc.—had begun to pall, and the sight of any rebellion, however puerile, however clumsy, roused up her partisanship. Since she could not shock Hallowby to its foundations, she liked to see these young creatures trying to, and wished them luck. From time to time she even made approaches to them, solicited their trust, indicated that she was ranged on their side. They accepted, confided, condescended—and dropped her.

When one is thus put back in one's place, one finds one has grown out of it, and is a misfit. Celia became conscious

how greatly she disliked Hallowby society. The school
people nauseated her with their cautious culture and breezy
heartiness. The indigenous inhabitants were more bear-
able, because they were less pretentious; but they bored
her. The Church, from visiting bishops down to Salvation
Army cornet players, she loathed for its hypocrisy. Only in
Hallowby's shabbiest quarter—in Edna Road, Gladstone
Terrace and Gas Lane—could she find anyone to love.
Mr. Newby the fishmonger in his malodorous den; old
Mrs. Foe among her sallowing cabbages and bruised
apples; Mr. Raby, the grocer, who couldn't afford to buy
new stock because he hadn't the heart to call in the money
his poorer customers owed him, and so had none but the
poorest customers—these people were good. Probably it
was only by their goodness that they survived and had not
cut their throats in despair long ago. Celia began to shop
in Gas Lane. It was not a success. Much as she might love
Mr. Newby she loved Justin better, and when a dried
haddock gave him food poisoning she had to remove her
custom—since the cat wouldn't touch Newby's fish
anyhow. These disheartening experiences made her
dislike respectable Hallowby even more. She wanted to
cast it off, as someone tossing in fever wants to cast off a
blanket.

The depression began. The increase of Mr. Raby's
customers drove him out of business: he went bankrupt
and closed the shop. Groups of unemployed men from
Hallowby juxta Mare appeared in Gas Lane and Edna
Road and sang at street corners—for misfortune always resorts to poor neighbourhoods for succour. People began to
worry about their investments and to cut down subscrip-
tions to such examples of conspicuous waste as the Chamber

Music Society. Experts on nutrition wrote to the daily papers, pointing out the wastefulness of frying, and explaining how, by buying cheaper cuts of meat and cooking them much longer, the mothers of families on the dole would be able to provide wholesome adequate meals. Celia's uneasy goodwill and smouldering resentment found their outlet. As impetuously as she had flung herself into Justin's bed, she flung herself into relief work at Hallowby juxta Mare. Being totally inexperienced in relief work she exploded there like a nova. Her schemes were so outrageous that people in authority didn't think them worth contesting even; she was left to learn by experience, and made the most of this valuable permission. One of her early outrages was to put on a revue composed and performed by local talent. Local talent ran to the impromptu, and when it became known what scarification of local reputations could be expected, everyone wanted to hear what might be said of everyone else and Celia was able to raise the price of admission, which had been sixpence, to as much as half a guinea for the best seats. Her doings became a joke; you never knew what that woman wouldn't be up to next. Hadn't she persuaded Wilson & Beck to take on men they had turned off, because now, when half the factory stood idle, was the moment to give it a spring cleaning? Celia worked herself to the bone, and probably did a considerable amount of good, but her great service to Hallowby juxta Mare was that she made the unemployed interested in their plight instead of dulled by it, so that helpers came to her from the unemployed themselves. If she was not so deeply impressed by their goodness as she had been by the idealized goodness of Mr. Newby and Mrs. Foe, she was impressed by their arguments; she became political, and by 1936 she was marching in Com munist demonstrations, singing:

> *Twenty-five years of hunger and war*
> *And they call it a glorious Jubilee.*

Inland Hallowby was also looking forward to the Jubilee. The school was rehearsing a curtailed version of Purcell's *King Arthur*, with Mary Semple, now home from her finishing school, coming on in a chariot to sing 'Fairest Isle'. There was to be folk dancing by Scouts and Guides, a tea for the old people, a fancy-dress procession; and to mark the occasion Mr. Harvey, J.P., one of the school governors, had presented the Beelby Museum with a pair of buckskin breeches worn by the Duke of Wellington on the field of Talavera. 'I shall be expected to make a speech about them,' groaned Justin. 'I think I shall hire a deputy and go away for the day.'

Celia jumped at this. 'We'll both go away. Not just for the day but for a fortnight. We'll go to Jersey, because you must attend the Jubilee celebrations on your native island —a family obligation. Representative of one of the oldest families. And if we find the same sort of fuss going on there, we can nip over to France in the Escudiers' boat and be quit of the whole thing. It's foolproof, it's perfect. The only thing needed to make it perfectly perfect is to make it a month. Justin, it's the answer.' She felt indeed that it was the answer. For some time now, Justin had seemed distrait and out of humour. Afraid he was unwell, she told herself he was stale and knew that he had been neglected. An escapade would put all right. Talavera had not been fought in vain. But she couldn't get him to consent. She was still persuading when the first letter arrived. It was typed and had been posted in Hallowby. It was unsigned, and began, 'Hag.'

Reading what followed, Celia tried to hold on to her first impression that the writer was some person in Hallowby juxta Mare. 'You think you're sitting pretty, don't you? You think no one has found you out.' She had made many enemies there; this must come from one of them. Several times she had been accused of misappropriating funds. Yes, that was it: '. . . and keep such a tight hold on him.' But why *him*? It was as though two letters lay on the flimsy page—the letter she was bent on reading and the letter that lay beneath and glared through it. It was a letter about her relations with Justin that she tore into bits and dropped in the wastepaper basket as he came down to breakfast.

She could hardly contain her impatience to get the bits out again, stick them on a backing sheet, make sure. Nothing is ever quite what it first was; the letter was viler, but it was also feebler. It struck her as amateurish.

The letter that came two days later was equally vile but better composed; the writer must be getting his or her hand in. A third was positively elegant. Vexatiously, there was no hint of a demand for hush money. Had there been, Celia could have called in the police, who would have set those ritual springes into which blackmailers—at any rate, blackmailers one reads of in newspapers—walk so artlessly. But the letters did not blackmail, did not even threaten. They stated that what the writer knew was common knowledge. After two letters, one on the heels of the other, which taunted Celia with being ugly, ageing and sexually ridiculous—letters that ripped through her self-control and made her cry with mortification—the writer returned to the theme of common knowledge and con-cluded with an 'It may interest you to hear that the follow-ing know all about your loathsome performances' and a list of half a dozen Hallowby names. Further letters laconically listed more names. From the outset, Celia had decided to keep all this to herself, and still held to the decision; but she hoped she wouldn't begin to talk in her sleep. There was less chance of this, as by now she was sleeping scarcely at all.

It was a Sunday morning and she and Justin were spraying roses for green-fly when Justin said, 'Puss, what are you concealing?' She syringed Mme. Alfred Carrière so violently that the jet bowed the rose, went beyond it, and deluged a robin. Justin took the syringe out of her hand and repeated the question.

Looking at him, she saw his face was drawn with woe. 'No, no, it's nothing like that,' she exclaimed. 'I'm perfectly well. It's just that some poison-pen imbecile . . .'

When he had read through the letters, he said thought-fully, 'I'd like to wring that little bitch's neck.'

'Yes, it is some woman or other, isn't it? I felt sure of that.'

'Some woman or other? It's Mary Semple.'

'That pretty little Mary Semple?'

'That pretty little Mary Semple. Give me the letters. I'll soon settle her.' He looked at his watch. 'No, I can't settle her yet. She'll still be in church.'

'But I don't understand why.'

'You do, really.'

'Justin! Have you been carrying on with Mary Semple?'

'No, I wouldn't say that. She's got white eyelashes. But ever since she came home Mary Semple has been doing all she could to carry on with me. There I was in the Beelby, you see, like a bull at the stake. No one comes near the place now; I was at her mercy. And in she tripped, and talked about the old days, telling me her little troubles, showing me poems, pitying me for my hard lot. I tried to cool her down, I tried to taper it off. But she was bent on rape, and one morning I lost all patience, told her she bored me and that if she came again I'd empty the fire bucket over her. She wept and wailed, and I paid no attention, and when there was silence I looked cautiously round and she was gone. And a day or so after'—he looked at the mended letter—'yes, a couple of days after, she sat her down to take it out of you.'

'But, Justin—how did she know about us?'

'No fire without smoke, I suppose. I dare say she overheard her parents cheering each other along the way with Christian surmises. Anyhow, children nowadays are brought up on that sort of useful knowledge.'

'No fire without smoke,' she repeated. 'And what about those lists?'

'Put in to make your flesh creep, most likely. Even if they do know, they weren't informed at a public meeting. Respectable individuals are too wary about libel and slander to raise their respectable voices individually. It's like that motet Pendarves used to talk about, when he could never manage to get them all there at once. Extraordinary ambitions people have! Fancy wanting to hear forty singers simultaneously yelling different tunes.'

'It can be done. There was a performance at Newcastle —he was dead by then. But, Justin——'

'That will do, Celia. I am now going off to settle Mary Semple.'

'How will you manage to see her alone?'

'I shall enter her father's dwelling. Mary will manage the rest.'

The savagery of these last words frightened her. She had not heard that note in his voice since he cried out in his sleep. She watched him limp from the room as though she were watching an incalculable stranger. A moment later he reappeared, took her hand, and kissed it. 'Don't worry, Puss. If need be, we'll fly the country.'

Whatever danger might lie ahead, it was the thought of the danger escaped that made her tremble. If she had gone on concealing those letters—and she had considered it her right and duty to do so—a wedge would have been driven between her and Justin, bruising the tissue of their love, invisibly fissuring them, as a wedge of ice does in the living tree. And thus a scandal about their incest would have found them without any spontaneity of reaction and distracted by the discovery of how long she had been arrogating to herself a thing that concerned them both. 'Here and now,' she exclaimed, 'I give up being an elder sister who knows best.' Justin, on his way to the Semples', was muttering to himself, 'Damn and blast it, why couldn't she have told me sooner? If she had it would all be over by now.' It did not occur to him to blame himself for a lack of openness. This did not occur to Celia, either. It was Justin's constancy that mattered, not his fidelity—which was his own business.

When he reappeared, washed and brushed and ready for lunch, and told her there would be no more billets-doux from Mary, it was with merely tactical curiosity that she asked, 'Did you have to bribe her?' And as he did not answer at once, she went on to ask, 'Would you like potted shrimps or mulligatawny? There's both.'

They did not have to fly the country. Mary Semple disposed of the rest of her feelings by quarrelling with everyone in the cast of *King Arthur* and singing 'Fairest Isle' with such venom that her hearers felt their blood run cold, and afterwards remarked that stage fright had made her sing out of tune. The people listed by Mary as cognizant showed no more interest in the Tizards than before. The tradesmen continued to deliver. Not a cold shoulder was turned. But on that Sunday morning the balance between Justin and Celia had shifted, and never returned to its former adjustment. Both of them were aware of this, so neither of them referred to it, though at first Celia's abdication made her rather insistent that Justin should know best, make decisions, assert his authority. Justin asserted his authority by knowing what decisions could be postponed till the moment when there was no need to make them at all. Though he did not dislike responsibility, he was not going to be a slave to it. Celia's abdication also released elements in her character which till then had been penned back by her habit of common sense and efficiency. She became slightly frivolous, forgetful and timid. She read novels before lunch, abandoned all social conscience about bores, mislaid bills, took second helpings of *risotto* and mashed potatoes and began to put on weight. She lost her aplomb as a driver and had one or two small accidents. She discovered the delights of needing to be taken away for pick-me-up holidays. Mrs. Mugthwaite, observing all this, knew it was the Change, and felt sorry for poor Mr. Tizard; the Change wasn't a thing that a brother should be expected to deal with. From time to time, Justin and Celia discussed leaving Hallowby and going to live somewhere away from the east-coast climate and the east wind at the corner by St. Cuthbert's, but they put off moving, because the two animals had grown old, were set in their ways, and would be happier dying in their own home. The pug died just before the Munich crisis, the cat lived on into the war.

So did Mr. Pilkington, who died from overwork two months before the first air raid on Hallowby juxta Mare justified his insistence on constructing an air-raid shelter under the school playing fields. This first raid was concentrated on the ironworks, and did considerable damage. All next day, inland Hallowby heard the growl of demolition explosives. In the second raid, the defences were better organized. The enemy bombers were driven off their target before they could finish their mission. Two were brought down out to sea. A third, twisting inland, jettisoned its remaining bombs on and around Hallowby. One dropped in Gas Lane, another just across the road from Newton Lodge. The blast brought down the roof and dislodged a chimney stack. The rescue workers, turning the light of their torches here and there, noting the usual disparities between the havocked and the unharmed, the fireplace blown out, the portrait smiling above it, followed the trail of bricks and rubble upstairs and into a bedroom whose door slanted from its hinges. A cold air met them; looking up, they saw the sky. The floor was deep in rubble; bits of broken masonry, clots of brickwork, stood up from it like rocks on a beach. A dark bulk crouched on the hearth, and was part of the chimney stack, and a torrent of slates had fallen on the bed, crushing the two bodies that lay there.

The wavering torchlights wandered over the spectacle. There was a silence. Then young Foe spoke out. 'He must have come in to comfort her. That's my opinion.' The others concurred. Silently, they disentangled Justin and Celia, and wrapped them in separate tarpaulin sheets. No word of what they had found got out. Foe's hypothesis was accepted by the coroner and became truth.

# SWANS ON AN
# AUTUMN RIVER

As he quitted the Aer Lingus plane from Liverpool and set foot for the first time in his life on Irish soil, he was already a disappointed man. He had promised himself a second caress of the stewardess's leg; but when the jostle of alighting passengers had brought him conveniently close to her she was standing pressed into the doorway, stiff as a ramrod, her shy, innocent looks which had been so particularly attractive changed for coldness and reserve. So there was nothing to be done. He put the intended tip back into his pocket and stepped off the plane a disappointed man. At his age, such disappointments are serious. You are only young once. At the time it seems endless, and is gone in a flash; and then for a very long time you are old.

Meanwhile, here he was, Norman Repton, aged sixty-nine, hearty as ever though overweight, attending a congress of sanitary engineers on behalf of the firm of Ingatestone & Murgatroyd. The invitation had not come to him. It had been handed on by Collins, the chairman of the board of management. 'You go, Norman. If you've never eaten a Dublin steak, you don't know what life is.' He had accepted, though as making a favour of it. He did not wish to admit to himself that at the thought of going to Ireland a long-outgrown desire had staggered to its feet. When he was young the notion of Ireland was romance to him. Its hills were bluer, its songs were sweeter. He knew 'The

Lake Isle of Innisfree' by heart. Later on he had tried to enlist in the Black and Tans. But after all, he could not have wanted to go to Ireland so very much, since he had never gone there.

There were some mountains on the skyline. Their shapes were graceful, but they were not particularly blue. Everywhere else was flattish, calm, dull, unexpectedly neat—though, of course, the pigs and the cabins and the red petticoats would have been expurgated from the vicinity of an airport—and composedly autumnal. A cold wind blew steadily from the west. It was not raining. It was not what he had meant.

Harvey Jessop was not what he had meant, either—that walking encyclopedia of facts and figures, a man whose presence would shrivel any sense of adventure. Nevertheless, recognizing his mincing gait and sloping shoulders among the group of passengers, now some way ahead, Norman Repton quickened his steps, caught up with him, hailed him.

'Hullo, Jessop! Going to the congress, too?'

'I didn't know you were coming.'

It was on the tip of his tongue to retort, 'Fancy there being anything you didn't know!' and at another time he would have said it; but now he did not want to alienate Jessop. With Jessop, one at least knew where one was. One couldn't be disillusioned in him. At Jessop's side he went through the customs, answered that he was over on a visit, was wished a pleasant stay. On Jessop's heels he went out through the glass doors.

'What about sharing a taxi?'

'Why? There's a bus.'

He sat down at Jessop's side. The bus started. The calm

landscape continued. They passed stone walls, then some startingly blue railings. They came into a region of small shops. The names above them were Irish names, with their rollicking associations: Dooley, Murphy, O'Flaherty. Some of the lettering had the classy illegibility he connected with expensive Christmas cards of a pious nature.

'What on earth does that say? I can't make head or tail of it.' Too late, Norman Repton realized that he had done what he had resolved not to do: he had admitted ignorance.

'Post Office. It's Erse. Erse is the official language.'

'Kathleen ni Houlihan, eh?'

Jessop began to speak of the economic drain of printing government forms in two languages. The road sloped downhill. Mountains appeared above the housetops—no doubt the same mountains he had seen from the airport, but suddenly so near, so sharply defined, that it was as though they had sprung up out of an ambush.

'Good Lord! What are those?' Norman Repton asked.

'The Dublin Mountains. They're quite useful. No worry about water supply.' They were gone again; the bus ran under a cliff of dark houses with long sashed windows and pillared doorways. The glass in the windows and the fanlights was broken. Here and there a dusky glimmer within showed that a roof was breached.

'What's happened to them? Was it a fire?'

'Tenements,' replied Jessop. 'Slums. The rich went, and the poor swarmed in. But soon even the rats will be leaving them.' He explained, with his facts and figures, how the population of central Dublin had fallen and that of its suburbs increased. 'That's where we come in, Repton. That's why I've come over for this congress. I want to know what's being done to see if we can't offer better terms.'

'You seem to have been making quite a study of it.'

'Naturally.'

At the bus terminal Jessop was still lecturing. Taking Norman Repton's arm he walked him past a Morgue and over a wide bridge where gulls were swirling like a snow flurry, talking about suburbs with mysterious names and growing populations demanding modern conveniences.

'But won't they smash them, like those windows?'

Jessop laughed. 'Not our affair, is it? In here.'

During lunch, it seemed increasingly plain that Jessop had designs on Ingatestone & Murgatroyd. A merger would indeed be something for Norman Repton to go back with; he wouldn't have come to Dublin for nothing. Presently he began to crow from his own dunghill. Crowing and drinking, they forgot the time and arrived twenty minutes late for the opening session. Their entry was frowned at—odd, in a country so notorious for its unpunctuality. But the oddity only glanced across Norman Repton's mind, for by now he had almost forgotten he was in Ireland. After the session, he asked Jessop to dine with him at his hotel. 'It's on Inns Quay, wherever that is.'

'I know it, I know it. Well, you'll be able to smell Guinness's brewery all right, in this wind. Yes, I'll come with pleasure, but I'll have to go early, I've got to go on somewhere else. You ought to go over Guinness's. They . . .'

Suddenly nettled, Norman Repton broke through Jessop's tale of hogsheads.

'I can't make it before seven-forty-five. I've got several things to do before then.'

In fact, he had nothing to do except to collect his suitcase from the terminal. This could wait till he had seen

something of Dublin. There was that view of the mountains—he liked a good view. As he was again on the north
bank of the river, all he need do, even if he could not re-
trace the way they had come in by, was to nose about for
a hill and walk up it.

But though he found himself walking rather exhaust-
ingly uphill, and coming to a curious region of wide un-
frequented streets and low terrace houses, shabbily genteel,
dominated by a portentously spiky church, the mountains
eluded him, for a mist was gathering and a muddied glow
of street lighting steamed up between him and them. What
he really wanted, after all, was a cup of tea, and he descended in search of it. Apparently this part of Dublin did
not go in for teashops, there were no notices saying
'Betty's Parlour'; no vistas of pink-lit rooms and little
tables; and suddenly he was out on the river again, in the
teeth of the wind. He let it carry him towards the bridge
he had earlier crossed with Jessop. The further side of the
river had seemed considerably more prosperous, holding
out more promise of pink-lit rooms and little tables and
somewhere to sit down in and possibly a pretty waitress.
A surge of hurrying people, sprung from nowhere, swept
him across the river, and while he still thought he knew
where he was going, he was borne on into a street that
frightened him. A railway crossed it, and quantities of
children with blackened faces darted in and out of alley-
ways, threatening each other with sparklers. It must have
been somewhere near the docks, for twice he heard the
melancholy lowing of a ship's hooter. Here and there were
groups of men who leaned against the lamp-posts and threw
down playing cards on the pavement, and once he passed an
old woman who sat on the kerb, rearranging the contents of

a shopping basket and benignly hiccuping, for she was drunk. But there was nowhere he could sit or lean, and the stupidity of fatigue drove him on until he saw a man going into a church, and followed him. Here at least he could sit down. Sit down he did. But it made him feel conspicuous, for the other people scattered about the building—and though nothing was happening there was quite a number of them—were on their knees. Roman Catholics, of course. He had nothing against them, but they made him feel awkward and a stranger. Candles were burning, some before this image, some before that. They gave a sort of top-dressing of warmth to the building, but basically it was as cold as river mud, and under a glazing of incense it smelt of poverty. Besides, how was he to get out? All those who went out crossed themselves, genuflected, even walked with a particular pious stealthiness. He could do none of these things, yet he did not want to offend. Looking at his watch, he realized that he must get out immediately, if he were to collect his suitcase and be in time for Jessop. At the terminal he got a taxi, saw the Morgue again, quite an old friend, and was at his hotel with five minutes to spare.

His room was on the second floor. The curtains had not been drawn across, and noticing this he noticed at the same time what seemed a rather unusual expanse of moonlit sky; and heard the rustle of the wind in a tree. The tree was on the pavement opposite. Beyond it was the breadth of river and the quay beyond. He had crossed the river four times already, but this was the first time he had really looked at it. It caught and dandled and polished the lights along the further embankment and from the pattern of the ripples in the reflections he got a perturbing impression that the river was flowing the wrong way. Then he remembered the nearness of the sea. It must be the incoming tide he saw, pushing the inland waters before it, driving them under the dark arches of the bridge. He would have liked to watch it longer, but the thought of Jessop took him downstairs.

He need not have left his window so soon, for Jessop was late. He came in with a hurried, disobliging air, complained of the cold, and said, as though he were talking to a child, 'Well, and how did you get on? How do you like Dublin?'

'There's one thing I couldn't make out. Why are all those children rushing about with sparklers and black faces? I wouldn't have expected Roman Catholics to go in for Guy Fawkes, somehow.'

'Halloween.'

'Halloween? But that's Scotch. Still, no reason why they shouldn't have it here, too. Scotch or Irish, eh? Which will you have to warm you up? I rather thought we'd have a bottle of Burgundy with our meal.'

They mixed grain and grape, they heaped roast duck on hot lobster.

'What's caragheen?' he asked the waitress, when she took away the duck.

'It's mawss.' She was a big tall woman, and she looked down on him maternally and spoke in a brooding, compassionate voice.

'Moss,' put in Jessop.

'Oh! Well, I don't think I'll have that. What'll you have, Jessop?'

'I won't have anything. I've got to be off. See you tomorrow.'

Left to himself, Repton ordered an omelet flambée, for

he wanted something that would invigorate him. Jessop had warmed up with the Burgundy, but even so it had been quite an effort to keep conversation going, and their fortuitous affability grew increasingly threadbare. It would have been easier with a younger waitress perhaps.

The omelet was slow in coming. He dozed off while waiting for it. It was a large omelet; they certainly didn't spare eggs in this country; but he got through it, looking at Jessop's crumbs and thinking they were better than his company. The room was emptying, extending, darkening; but a steady rattle of conversation persisted from a family party some tables away—all of them, except for two silent little girls, discussing some sort of lawsuit. Silly to keep children up so late. He ordered coffee and a brandy.

'Your coffee, sir.'

'Eh? What's that, what's that?'

He heard his own voice, sounding loud and abrupt, opened his eyes, saw that the family party had somehow gone away, and fell asleep again, slumped in his chair, his head sinking forward, his hands relaxed on his thighs.

A change came over him. Sitting there in his heavy ruinous estate of age and joylessness, with all his grossness exposed and defenceless, he began to look almost noble. It was as though an artist had made him, and not he himself.

'He's old, God help him!' said the big waitress. 'And anyway, it was the other one was the blackguard.'

'Will you be sitting up with him?' asked the cashier, locking her desk with a flourish.

'I'll leave him a bit longer. He's doing no harm.'

In the end, he was awakened, and the porter took him up to his room, and put him to bed. Just as he was going, Norman Repton said, 'Draw back those curtains.'

'Yes, sir.'

'Might want to look at the river.'

It seemed that to get out of bed and look at the river would in some way re-establish him and make up for the failure of the evening—the failure to hook Jessop, to digest the omelet, to have enjoyed himself either with a view of mountains, a cup of tea when he wanted it, the stewardess's young leg, a first day in a city that once, a long time ago, had been romantic and unattainable. In fact, he would not have needed to get out of bed. It would have been sufficient to look at the ceiling, where the river was casting its lightly dancing image. But this he did not know, sucked down into his heavy sleep. He spent an uneasy night, at the mercy of his digestion and his bladder, trying to crawl back into sleep like an animal into its lair, indifferent to the river outside, unaware of its counterpart dancing so lightly overhead. Then, when at last he was sleeping restfully, a great bell stripped him naked, as his father used to do, pulling back the blankets and threatening to empty the jug over him. Its loud, stark strokes seemed to march into the very room, at the same time unloosing bells all over the city, each of them reiterating its single note, except for a carillon which chimed out a hymn tune whose pinched intonation and jigging rhythm called up in his mind a picture of some bedizened spinster. But his indigestion was gone, and the noise of renewing traffic and of people moving about in the hotel encouraged him with the thought that yesterday's disappointments were behind him, and that here was another day, which might be a more satisfactory one. It promised to be a fine day, too. Light was welling upwards, lifting a tenuous web of cloud and here and there beginning to break it; broken, it took on a perceptible movement, a convoy of clouds sailing eastwards. The wind of yesterday, but lessened. He had no objection to a slight wind; it was even rather pleasant, and made one feel brisk. Colour grew in the plane tree outside. The wind fluttered its dwindled stock of leaves but did not detach them. Behind the plane tree, on the farther bank of the river, was an expanse of housefront painted a bright clear shade of yellow. It looked quite Continental. His eye rested on it with pleasure. He was, after all, waking up in what was almost a foreign city. He hoisted himself from his bed, walked across to the window and looked out. Over the undulating reflection of the yellow house floated two swans. Presently, from under the dark arch of the bridge came another swan, and, presently, another. While he was watching and admiring, three more swans appeared, moving into mid-stream from the near bank, where the quay's parapet had concealed them. Seven swans . . . That was something, and a lovely sight. A bus came along the quay, and paused, blocking out the river. When it moved on, he counted the swans as though they were his hoard, his treasure. There were now eleven swans. As he counted them again, to make sure, another sailed out from under the bridge.

They were making their way downstream, but dallied, oaring about to inspect floating bits of rubbish, diving their long necks below the surface with a burrowing motion, scavenging with unruffled classical dignity. He hurried into his clothes. Unwashed, unshaved, his shoes untied, he stumbled downstairs. In the hall, an idea occurred to him. He turned into the dining room, where a thin young man was already breakfasting, served by the big waitress. 'Bread!' he shouted. 'I want some bread.' As she came forward, his glance fell on a row of plated breadbaskets, ranged on the sideboard. He shovelled the sliced bread from half a dozen of these into one basket, and hurried on out, saying over his shoulder, 'It's all right. I'll pay for it.'

The *garda* directing the traffic by the bridge shouted a warning to him as he scrambled across the road under the nose of a lorry. A group of women waiting for a bus stepped quickly out of his path. It seemed an age before he could look over the parapet. Some of the swans had moved downstream, but others had arrived. Fifteen, sixteen, seventeen . . . there were eighteen swans. What a total! What a boast! 'In Dublin I've seen eighteen swans within a stone's throw.' Drawing a breath that cost him agony, he whistled. They paid no attention. 'Swans!' he hallooed. 'Swans!' One near by seemed to be looking at him from its sidewise face. He threw a slice of bread at it. It turned. Others turned. They came flocking towards him. Even in the wildness of his excitement and sense of personal glory he admired how skilfully they shaped their course without check or collision and how, as he scattered the bread among them, they went after it and contested for it with an air of proud negligence, feeding, he said to himself, like lords. He was about to throw in the last slice of bread when it was twitched from his hand, and in an instant the air between him and the river was shaken and noisy with gulls. Flapping, disputing, wheeling round and round, the ugly, greedy, bullying creatures were attacking his swans and stealing their bread. 'Get out!' he shouted. 'Get out, you brutes! Damn you, damn you, damn you, you dirty bastards!' Shaking with rage, he hurled the breadbasket into the midst of them. They thinned for a moment, and he saw that the swans had drawn away towards the opposite bank, and were heading downstream.

His rage came up in his throat and choked him. He lost all thought of who he was or where he was, and the hand clenching and unclenching on the rim of the parapet might have been the hand of a stranger. A bit of bread lay beside it. A gull, flying belatedly after the others, saw the bit, and swooped down. He struck at the gull with all his force, missed it, lost his balance, struggled to regain it, and fell backwards, his head striking the pavement. A terrified giggle broke from one of the women and was peremptorily hushed by another. For a while he struggled, threshing about with violent, unco-ordinated movements. The woman who had giggled moved diffidently forward, meaning to help him up. 'Best leave him alone,' said the woman who had silenced her. The voice was not so much harsh as harshly resigned. She had known much trouble in her life, and this had left her with no sympathy to spare for a corpulent old Englishman who had thrown a breadbasket into the Liffey and cursed the hungry seagulls—nor, indeed, for the seagulls either. She need not have spoken. Frightened by the grimace frozen on the old man's features, and by his set, snarling lips, the other had stopped short.

The *garda*, who had left his place amid the traffic, now came up to where Norman Repton lay motionless. After a momentary hesitation, as though he were hastily summoning up something he had learned, he knelt beside him. The women drew closer together, and one of them pulled her coat about her, as though she had suddenly become conscious of the cold. Presently the *garda* looked up. 'Will one of you ladies go across to the hotel,' he said, 'and ask them to telephone for the ambulance?' Two women detached themselves from the group and hurried across the road, arguing in whispers.

# THE VIEW OF ROME

FROM that morning when he woke to the sound of the first autumnal gale lashing like a caged tiger against the house fronts and knew with physical infallibility that after all he was going to recover, Guy Stoat burned with impatience to get out of the County Hospital and go home. He burned with an inward fire. He had never been a man to canvass attention or make a display of his feelings, even to himself—and a man can as easily be blinded by his own feelings as deafened by those of others. Guy's impatience did not blind him; it sharpened his sight and concentrated it on his objective. As through that keyhole in the massive door on the Aventine through which one stares in fascination at the view of Rome, till the remainder of one's gazing self seems to have been left hanging on the door like a coat, Guy saw his small magpie house, whose warping timber frame had pulled it a little off the straight, and the two yew trees shaped into cockyolly birds and the flagged path running between them to the door which he would open with his key and shut behind him. Fortunately, he had finished clipping the yews before his stomach ulcer had tripped him. If he got back by the beginning of October, and dodged the silly daylight-saving by getting up an hour earlier, he would have the garden combed and tidied before he settled down for the winter.

But, of course, at this juncture the hospital took it into its head to thwart him. Hitherto, he had been assured that he was making quite remarkable progress, that he would soon be feeling more like himself every day, that it was only a question of time. Now he was told that recovery was bound to be slow, especially in a man of his age, that he must not expect to run before he could walk, that it was all a question of patience and due course. When they were assuring him of his remarkable progress, he had felt too weak to contradict. He did not contradict now; he had better things to save his strength for. He lay still, and husbanded his impatience, and Sister Lockwood said at intervals, 'You're really quite a model patient, Mr. Stoat.' The night nurse in charge of the private ward was called Considine. Night relaxes discipline, and by 3 a.m. Sister Considine became almost human. She would drink a cup of tea at his bedside, and once they had a quite rational conversation about owls. One comes to feel a certain degree of security with a woman whose aunt had slept in a fourposter with a tame owl perched on the rail, and though Guy knew better than to mention his impatience to leave the hospital, one night he went so far as to admit that he had a home and was attached to it.

'I ought to be making apple jelly at this moment,' he remarked wistfully.

'Not quite at this moment, Mr. Stoat, surely.'

Poor wretch, who would never get away, she must be allowed her titter. The summoning light glowed, the titter was cut short, and Sister Considine went on to another patient.

Living from night to night as other people live from day to day, when next she saw him she took up where they had left off. 'Do you like making apple jelly, Mr. Stoat? It's rather an unusual passion for a gentleman.'

'I prefer making damson cheese. Did your aunt make damson cheese?'

(A dark, slow process, compatible with owls on a four-poster.)

'I don't seem to remember her having anything to do with damsons. She went in more for embroidery.'

(Pallas Athene, of course, mistress of her needle.)

Finding that he was about to fall impolitely asleep, neither in the aunt's fourposter nor in the metal contraption that raised him aloft as though on a sacrificial altar but in his own dear bed at home, Guy roused himself and said, 'I can't compete in embroidery. But I can do a good darn when I give my mind to it.'

'Can you really? Well, of course, it's useful for a bachelor to know how to darn. Though I hope you don't often have to darn, Mr. Stoat.'

'I do all my own darning.'

'Socks,' said she, understandingly.

'Not only socks. Sheets, towels. I can wash, too, and iron.'

(The washing line under the apple trees. The smell of linen when frost has stiffened it, taken down from the line on a still, green-skied evening. The ironing board's place under the stairs, and the mat just inside the kitchen door where his gardening shoes were faithfully awaiting him.)

'But do you live all alone, Mr. Stoat? Will there be no one to look after you when we send you back?'

(Her back arching under his hand, the soft treading paws.)

'There'll be——' Sleepwalking on the edge of the pit, he opened his eyes just in time and saw the gaping danger. These hospital know-it-alls would never accept a cat as an adequate companion for a convalescent—'Hattie,' he continued unswervingly. 'My step-niece. She's coming to spend the winter with me.'

'That's good news. It would never have done for you to be all alone.'

'No, no. I agree. Fortunately, there'll be Hattie.'

When they were making him ready for the operating theatre, drawing on white woollen stockings that clustered round his legs like a swarm of bees, someone had appeared with a form for which he had to supply answers. 'Occupation: wood engraver. Next of kin. . . .' Who had he named? He remembered deciding against Bartle, and against Joanna. He certainly hadn't named Hattie, though his cat was more to him than ten thousand Joannas. However, he had named her now.

'She's a dear domesticated little thing,' he said. This somehow lacked the ring of truth; at any rate, it was not the sort of phrase he had ever employed before. 'She's coming from the Isle of Wight.'

That sounded better. Conscious that his heart was beating vehemently and that his hands were tending to claw the sheet he said no more, and presently Sister Considine went away.

As he had expected, next morning Sister Lockwood had learned from Sister Considine that he was not going home to a solitary life—which, of course, would never have done. Observing how few visitors he had, and none of them ladies, Sister Lockwood had begun to feel quite worried about who would be there to look after him. Once again, he domiciled Hattie in the Isle of Wight—too far away for visiting him in the hospital, but she would come when she was needed. As he spoke, a further advantage about the Isle of Wight flashed into his mind and he added that she had a little cottage at Bonchurch. Milllard, of the Satyr Press, for whom he had been doing a set of woodcuts for *Hudibras* till pain wrenched the graver from his hand, lived at Bonchurch, and Mullard's reply to his recent letter of explanation and assurances that the woodcuts would be got on with as soon as he was let out should come shortly. Mullard's dainty calligraphy on an envelope could easily be mistaken for a woman's hand.

'And that's something I must ask you about. My niece—she's my step-niece, really . . .'

'Quite an unusual relationship!'

'Yes. But very convenient just now. My step-niece will have to pack up and settle things and find someone to look after her canaries before leaving the Island. I must be able to give her some idea of the date when I shall be leaving here.'

'Oh, Mr. Stoat, I can't possibly do that. That is for Dr. Jones to decide.' Her manner implied that Guy had asked her to commit some grave impropriety—which, however, she would undertake as consentingly as a temple slave if Dr. Jones ordained it.

Mullard's letter came two days later. The fact that Mullard didn't see what could be done if the blocks weren't in the printers' hands before the New Year should have had more weight than those canaries. But instinct told Guy that it would be imprudent to imply any existence other than that of being a patient in the County Hospital. He left the envelope—luckily, the postmark was boldly stamped—on his bed table, and when next Dr. Jones came in to look at him he repeated the sentence about Hattie; omitting the canaries, which he judged might here be inopportune.

'Hmm. Ah. Ha. Well. Well, if you continue to gain strength, and if no undesirable contra-indications arise, I dare say that in another couple of weeks I may be able to give you some idea when we shall be in a position to think about letting you go.'

'Don't do it too suddenly.'

'There will be no suddenness.'

Guy would have preferred a little suddenness. Time, no doubt, would have allowed him to build Hattie up into a more interesting figure, to give her volume and movement and that something which distinguishes the considered work of art from the impromptu, however spirited. But he did not wish to make her too interesting, lest he compromised the original outline. In any case, their Hattie was nothing to him. All he wanted was to get home, sleep in his own bed, and eat his own cooking. When next he wrote to Mullard . . . Good God! It flashed on him that there was something a great deal more vital than that. He must write to Hattie! Whether or no he gave Hattie volume and movement, he must demonstrably be in communication with her, he must give her a surname and a local habitation and a postage stamp. Some ordinary, unalarming surname, like Jones, would probably be best—though not Jones, which might seem too much of a coincidence. When one comes to reflect on it, it is extraordinary how seldom one meets anybody called Jones. But the telephone directory bears out the existence of multitudinous Browns, and a letter addressed to Miss H. Brown, Bonchurch, Isle of Wight, might be expected to reach one among the many who, reading its trivial contents (*'Dear Friend. It seems a long time since I heard from you. How is your mother? What wretched weather we are having. I suppose we shall soon be thinking about Christmas. Do write when you have time. Yours, G.S.'*), might equally be expected to drop it in a wastepaper basket; whereas a letter to Miss Harriet Maulererer might just as likely ricochet back on him with a 'Not Known. Opened by the Postal Authorities' all over the envelope. He had just realized that this could be averted if he wrote without giving his address when the bed table was swung briskly past his chin and a tray put down on it, holding foodstuffs of the variety known to dietitians as bland and to the common people as mush. But eat he must. Every blandishment left unconsumed would delay the hour of his dismissal.

Dissatisfaction is a mildew, and creeps. His dissatisfaction with what he was eating crept on to what he had been thinking, and letters whether to Miss Brown or Miss Mauleverer seemed alike otiose. Otiose or dangerous: it is proverbially dangerous to prod up the unknown. Think of the Witch of Endor. He was thinking of the Witch of Endor when a light from Heaven was vouchsafed. Who was that woman Mullard had taken him to lunch with, and who gave them such uncommonly good coffee in a very Victorian conservatory? Something Mackenzie. Morag Mackenzie. And her house was called Tir nan Og. Nothing could be better! The letter M can easily be stylized to resemble the letter H. All he now needed was a pretext. As the lunch had been eaten some years ago, it was late in the day to thank her for the coffee, even though it lingered in the memory. But there was not all that Celtic Twilight for nothing. Morag Mackenzie supported Island and Highland industries; there had been a quantity of parti-coloured knitted garments lying on a sofa, and Mullard had commissioned a sweater. When the tray was removed,

Guy wrote to Miss Mackenzie saying that he wanted a moorit cardigan, and that his measurements were about ordinary. He added that he had been ill, and expected to be home soon, feeling the cold. When next Sister Lockwood came round, the letter was in the envelope, the envelope was addressed and his stamp book was safely mislaid between the blankets.

'If you could stamp it for me, Sister, so that it catches the afternoon post . . . It's to my step-niece Hattie, who's coming to look after me. I'm asking her to knit me a warm cardigan, to wear when I get back. I felt this was a sensible thing to do.'

The deed was approved, the letter borne off: Guy retrieved the stamp book and lay back on his pillows, reposing in the thought of a step taken and the unities preserved. He had not a drop of Scottish blood; but that was no reason why Hattie should not be Mackenzie—she was a stepniece. After all this plotting and scheming on Hattie's behalf, she was becoming quite real to him. He thought of her as small yet plump, unconversational, light-footed and wearing grey, with green eyes. Early in the next week, the cardigan also became more of a reality to him. Miss Mackenzie sent him a measurement form.

Guy now ran up against the sterner aspects of the welfare state, for it appeared that the National Health Service made no provision for hospitalized persons requiring tape measures. At first replying that she would see, Sister Lockwood, when next invoked, said coldly, 'I'm sorry, Mr. Stoat. We have no tape measure.' The transition to the first person plural told him to hope no more—it was clear that in this instance she would not even ask Dr. Jones about it. Sister Considine, who might have yielded so far as to think of a tape measure inherited from her aunt, was not on night duty that week. The nurse who replaced her was young, high-coloured and wore glasses. Her reaction to his request was to take his temperature, looking at him the while as if she knew all about that sort of thing. However, there was still the old woman in an overall who came every morning to sweep his floor and move his belongings out of reach. She was not cloistered in professionalism, so she might be more complying.

'Well, that's a funny article for a gentleman to ask for. I've been asked for a lot of funny articles, one time and another, but never for that. There was one poor lady, I remember, she was in for that op. when they sweep it all away, you understand, and naturally, I dare say, it made her imaginative. Well, what she imagined was a mouse that kept on gnawing the leg of her bed—which is a thing no mouse would have done, even if there'd been a mouse, being every inch of it metal. And in the mornings she'd say, "Oh, Mrs. Bolton," she'd say, "the way that mouse keeps on gnawing is chronic. Can't you get me a mouse-trap?"'

'So you did. I'm sure you did,' said Guy, hopefully seeking to inflame the warmth of Mrs. Bolton's heart.

'No, sir, I can't say that. I've got my Annie to think of, I can't risk the sack. Bringing things in is strictly against orders, and once you start giving way, you never know where it mayn't land you. Not that with private beds there isn't more latitude than in the wards. Which with all respect to you, as being a member of the Women's Co-operative, I cannot say I hold with. Nor never have. Death's a leveller. And so ought any self-respecting hospital to be, seeing as in most cases you might describe it as death's door. They're bringing them in from Birmingham now.'

The last hope of the tape measure seemed to be sliding from his grasp.

'From Birmingham, Mrs. Bolton?'

'The influenza epidemic. It's come early this year. But I'm not surprised, I've never seen such hordes of wood lice. Well, I'm prepared for it. I've gone into my winter combies already.'

'That's very wise of you. More wool, fewer shrouds . . . It's an old saying.'

'And a true one.'

'That is why I want a tape measure. You see, my step-niece, who lives in the Isle of Wight——'

'Oh, was that why you wanted it? Well now, there might be one in Matron's cupboard. But I can't ask her. Matron's Matron.'

'Exactly. And with all these cases coming in from Birmingham——'

'Yes. It's a poor lookout.' Mrs. Bolton paused and surveyed the poor lookout.

'I'll tell you what I'll do. I'll ask Howard, the porter. I saw him measuring something only the other day.'

She came back with a carpenter's rule. By combining this with his handkerchief, Guy managed to fill out the measurement form, while Mrs. Bolton stood by, urging him to look sharp about it. It was a scramble, and it left him breathless and dizzy. Home had never seemed farther off. I shall have a relapse, he thought. I shall never get away. . . . There is a stage in convalescence when the sensation of returning health is replaced by the sensation of being far from well. Guy was in it now, and felt it badly.

Instead of having a relapse, that afternoon he had a visitor, the rector's wife, who explained that as she had had to come in to see the dentist she had come to see him, too. 'The buses,' she continued, 'run so awkwardly, and the Rector needed the car.' She then sat down with her knees together and her feet apart, and looked at him attentively. 'I don't think you're looking very well.'

In a cautious, private way, Guy rather liked Mrs. Oke. 'It's because I have been pining,' he said. 'Tell me all the news. Tell me about the Harvest Festival.'

'But didn't you read about poor Canon Urchfont? It was all most unfortunate. There were far too many apples. There always are. And this year there were far too many wasps. And one of them stung Canon Urchfont and he died of it. We were all very sad. What do they call it when you die of something you wouldn't have been so likely to die of if you did something else?'

'Occupational risk.'

'I wonder how you know all these things. You lead a totally selfish life, you never go beyond your own gate and yet you know about occupational risks. Well, I suppose dying of a wasp at a Harvest Festival might be considered an occupational risk for a Rural Dean. Have you heard that Violet Dancer has married?'

'No! Who to?'

'Ellery Price. It's made a great difference to the post office, because now it's full of his dogs. Some people don't like it—people with dogs of their own, who take them in.'

'How many dogs?'

'Seven.'

'What on earth do they feed them on?'

'Dog biscuit.'

(And how is my darling house that I shall never see again?)

Mrs. Oke, rising to depart, said, 'I suppose I shall be coming in any day now to fetch you. I told the almoner that you would much rather come out by taxi, but apparently you must have someone with you in case you faint. I expect they want your bed.'

Even with these intimations, Guy was taken aback when a couple of days later they told him he had better get up in the afternoon and walk about a little, as he would be going out on the morrow.

'But don't pack,' said Sister Lockwood. 'You will have plenty of time to do that in the morning, as Mrs. Oke can't come for you till half past three. I suppose that niece of yours will be there to put you to bed when you arrive?'

His temper rising, Guy said, 'How can she be, since she's in the Isle of Wight?'

'Oh, is she? I thought she lived at Stratford-on-Avon. Well, you must send her a telegram. Write it out now and the office will telephone it.'

They were determined enough to get rid of him. Even so, his freedom seemed to hang on Hattie. So what the devil was he to telegraph to Morag Mackenzie, with whom his only link was a woollen one? FIND MY ARMS ARE TWO INCHES LONGER, STOAT. Curbing such flights of fancy, he wrote: 'LEAVING HOSPITAL TOMORROW.' Morag Mackenzie might think this rather gushing. On the other hand, she might put it down to efficiency. Efficient people are always sending needless telegrams.

Sitting in the car with Mrs. Oke's conversation playing over him like an unemphatic east wind he fingered his latch key, but didn't get much comfort from it. The view through the keyhole had somehow lost its lighting, its magic, its compactness. It had fallen to pieces, riddled by obligations. The parsley would have run to seed. The tools would be rusty. He would have to get the chimney sweep.

'I hope your house won't be very damp. Mrs. Lugg has been in every day this week, lighting fires and airing it.'

If that was the case, by now it was probably a heap of ashes. Well, there were other houses. When one has grown old, there is something to be said for living in a bungalow on a bus route. At the crossroads, Mrs. Oke drove straight on. He made no comment. She, too, might well have lost interest in going home.

'Mrs. Lugg told me she'd got in what food you'll need —and a nice bit of steak off the butcher's van. So we'll go round by Buckleford, and find something edible at Paytoe's. You can give the steak to the cat. Has the hospital left you with enough money for a partridge, or would you feel safer with a dozen oysters?'

Partridges need roasting, oysters have to be opened. 'I think I'll make do with a boiled egg.'

Nevertheless, she forced housekeeping upon him and having parked him outside the churchyard came back with a load of parcels, all of which he supposed he would have to deal with. He felt like a parcel himself—except that a parcel would not have blenched at Mrs. Oke's fatalistic way of driving. Now she stopped on a sharp bend, opened the driver's window and beckoned up a woman on a bicycle. A smell of wood smoke drifted into the car. His impatience blazed up out of its ashes and for the remainder of the journey he could barely contain his excitement. She turned up the lane; a group of village children scattered before her, a blackbird flew screeching out of the hedge.

There, behind its yew-tree birds, was his magpie house. Remembering to thank her, he got out and opened his gate, noting that the hinges could do with some oil.

'I'll help you with your things,' she said. If it had not been for that idiotic shopping, he could have managed perfectly well. But he submitted, thanking her again. She preceded him to the door, where she put down her load. 'I'm not coming any farther.' This time, he thanked her unfeignedly.

He let himself in, and was home.

Yet between him and his realization of return was a brittle transparent film, like cat ice—the remembrance of taking leave. It was as though he had broken in on Guy Stoat waiting for the ambulance, an old man writhing in the claws of pain and fear, who shuffled to and fro, expending his last minutes in an obsessed determination to leave everything in order. And on the whole the old man hadn't done too badly. It looked right and tight, though on closer examination such details as the pepper grinder on the window sill, stationed exactly midway between the pair of white Dresden swans, betrayed a distracted mind pressganging a steady hand. He carried the pepper grinder into the kitchen. This, being less mortally neat, was better. His gardening shoes were on their mat (the other Guy Stoat had given them a sound brushing), the tea tray was laid, the kettle filled. While it boiled, he read the note that Mrs. Lugg had left on the tray: 'Dear Mr. Stoat. Welcome home I'm sure, hope you find all satisfactory, I'll be back as soon as I've seen to Lugg's tea. Yours truly (Mrs.) Rosie M. Lugg.' He drank his tea walking about the kitchen, and if he had been a superstitious man he would have poured a libation beside his gardening shoes. The clock with its light hopping gait, like a robin's, ticked on. He waited. Then the back door opened and Mrs. Lugg came in, carrying a wicker hamper.

'Well, Mr. Stoat, glad to see you home again. I've brought up Hattie.' She raised the lid of the hamper. A grey cat jumped out, gave him a quick glance, turned her back on him and began to sharpen her claws on a table leg.

'I hope she's been good, and no trouble to you.'

'Oh, no! It's been a pleasure to have her. She's a dear clean little thing—and doesn't she go after the mice!'

Hattie was now on the window sill, spitting out geranium leaves and threatening to hurl the flower pots to the floor.

'She wants to run out and have a look round,' Mrs. Lugg remarked. 'I dare say you do, too, after being away so long.' In case this was not plain enough, she set the back door open before gathering up the tea things and putting them in the sink.

At the back of the house was a stretch of rough grass, where gnarled apple trees stood about like aged men, their limbs supported by wooden props. At his first step, he trod on an apple. With the second step, he trod on another. Wherever he looked, the ground was a mosaic of fallen apples ('I ought to be making apple jelly at this moment'). Beyond the orchard was a jungle. A frieze of towering acanthus fronds dominated it, like a last assertion of classical thought foundering amid the Dark Ages. In fact, it was the artichoke row at the foot of the kitchen garden. Hattie had frisked up a tree and was disporting herself overhead. Now she dislodged some more apples, which hit him on the back. She sprang into the neighbouring tree, and yellow apples fell instead of crimson ones. Apple jelly, forsooth! Tilth and order, and summer's trailing rags disposed of in bonfires and compost heaps! Here he stood, in the fourth week of October, with nothing performed except the cockyolly birds. Even if he had known where to begin, it was too late for beginning.

'I've finished,' came Mrs. Lugg's voice from the doorway. 'So if it's all the same to you, I'll be getting back.'

Her footsteps echoed along the flagged path, were muted in the muddy lane, died away. There was a rip of claws slicing through lichen, and a softer, more living thud on the grass. Hattie was at his feet, rolling among the apples. He picked her up.

'My dear Hattie, you don't know what lies I've been telling about you. I said you kept canaries. I said you lived on an island, knitting.'

She squirmed out of his arms onto his shoulder, and began to rub the top of her head against his cheek, purring as though the world contained no pleasure comparable to this, for which she had been waiting in silence and reserve ever since that woman had thrust her into a hamper.

'We've both suffered a great deal of ignominy, my dear. I wouldn't think of offering you tough steak on a night like this. We will dine on partridge.'

Her purr and her warmth and her softness seemed to pull the dusk down over them. Already a light frost was stiffening the grass as he carried her indoors, turning his back on obligations that he would probably ignore. There had never been such an apple year. Canon Urchfont had died of it. Quite possibly this was what had been intended. God is an Oriental potentate, unaffectedly lavish and sumptuous. He would not think it extravagant to heap up all these apples into a cenotaph for a Rural Dean. Here was no need for jampots. They could stay in the attic.

# AN ACT OF REPARATION

Lapsang sooshang—must smell like tar.
Liver salts in *blue* bottle.
Strumpshaw's bill—why 6*d*.?
Crumpets.
Waistcoat buttons.
Something for weekend—not a chicken.

So much of the list had been scratched off that this remainder would have made cheerful reading if it had not
been for the last item.

Valerie Hardcastle knew where she was with a chicken.
You thawed it, put a lump of marg inside, and roasted it.
While it was in the oven you could give your mind to
mashed potatoes (Fenton couldn't endure packet crisps),
bread sauce and the vegetable of the season—which lat-
terly had been sprouts. A chicken was calm and straightforward: you ate it hot, then you ate it cold; and it was a
further advantage that one chicken is pretty much like
another. Chicken is reliable—there is no apple-pie-bed
side to its character. With so much in married life proving
apple-pie-beddish, the weekend chicken had been as soothing as going to church might be if you were that sort of
person. But now Fenton had turned—like any worm, she
thought, though conscious that the comparison was inadequate—declaring that he was surfeited with roast

chicken, that never again was she to put one of those wretched commercialized birds before him.

'Think of their hideous lives, child! Penned up, regimented, stultified. They never see a blade of grass, they never feel the fresh air, all they know is chicken, chicken, chicken—just like us at weekends. Where is that appalling draught coming from? You must have left a window open somewhere.'

'What do you think I ought to get instead? I could do liver-and-bacon. But that doesn't go on to the next day.'

'Can't you get a joint?'

A joint. What joint? She had never cooked a joint. At home, Mum made stews. At the Secretarial College there was mince and shepherd's pie. No doubt a joint loomed in the background of these—but distantly, like mountains in Wales. When she and Olive Petty broke away from the college to share a bed-sitting room and work as dancing partners at the town's new skating rink their meals mainly consisted of chips and salami, varied by the largesse of admirers who took them to restaurants. Fenton, as an admirer, had expressed himself in *scampi* and *crêpes Suzette*— pronounced 'crapes', not 'creeps'—with never a mention of joints. Grey-haired, though with lots of it, he was the educated type, and theirs was an ideal relationship till Mrs. Fenton, whom he had not mentioned either—not to speak of—burst out like a tiger, demanding divorce. The case was undefended. Six months later to the day, Fenton made an honest woman of her. Brought her down to earth, so to speak.

Marriage, said the registrar, was a matter of give-and-take. Marriage, thought Valerie, was one thing after another. Now it was joints. Sunk in marriage, she sat at a small polished table in the bank, waiting for Fenton's queries about his statement sheets to be thoroughly gone into, meanwhile enjoying the orderliness and impersonality of an establishment so unlike a kitchen or a bedroom.

And at an adjoining table sat the previous Mrs. Hardcastle who for her part had come to withdraw a silver teapot from the bank's strong room, examining with a curiosity she tried to keep purely abstract the young person who had supplanted her in Fenton's affections. Try as she might, abstraction was not possible. Conscience intervened, compunction and stirrings of guilt. It was all very well for Isaac; he had not drawn Abraham's attention to the ram in the thicket. It was all very well for Iphigenia, who had not suggested to the goddess that a hind could replace her at the sacrificial altar. Isaac and Iphigenia could walk off with minds untroubled by any shade of responsibility for the substituted victim. But she, Lois Hardcastle, writhing in the boredom of being married to Fenton, had snatched at Miss Valerie Fry, who had done her no harm whatever, and got away at her expense. And this, this careworn, deflated little chit staring blankly at a shopping list, was what Fenton had made of her in less than six months' matrimony.

'Oh, dear!' said Lois, and sighed feelingly.

Hearing the exclamation and the sigh, Valerie glanced up to discover who was taking on so. She could see nothing to account for it. The woman was definitely middle-aged, long past having anything to sound tragic about. Indeed, she looked uncommonly healthy and prosperous, was expensively made up, wore a wedding ring, had no shopping bags—so why should she jar the polish and repose of a bank by sighing and exclaiming 'Oh dear?' Leg of lamb, leg of pork, leg of . . . did nothing else have legs? A bank clerk came up with a sealed parcel, saying 'Here it is, Mrs. Hardcastle. If you'll just sign for it.'

'Here, you've made a mistake! Those aren't Mr. Hardcastle's——' As Valerie spoke, she saw the parcel set down in front of the other woman. Fenton's other one. For it was she, though so smartened up as to be almost unrecognizable. What an awkward situation! And what a pity she had drawn attention to herself by saying that about the parcel. Fortunately, Fenton's other one did not appear to have noticed anything. She read the form carefully through, took her time over signing it, exchanged a few words with the clerk about the time of year before he carried it away. Of course, at her age she was probably a bit deaf, so she would not have heard those give-away words. The give-away words sounded on in Valerie's head. She was still blushing vehemently when the other Mrs. Hardcastle looked her full in the face and said, cool as a cucumber, 'Mrs. Lois Hardcastle, now. What an odd place we've chosen to meet in.'

Pulling herself together, Valerie replied, 'Quite a co-incidence.'

'Such a small world. I've come to collect a teapot. And you, I gather, are waiting for Fenton's statement sheets, just as I used to do. And it's taking a long time, just as it always did.'

'There were some things Mr. Hardcastle wanted looked into.'

Not to be put down, Mr. Hardcastle's earlier wife continued, 'Now that the bank has brought us together, I hope you'll come and have coffee with me. I'm going back to London tonight, so it's my only chance to hear how you both are.'

'I don't know that I can spare the time, thank you all the same, I'm behindhand as it is, and I've got to buy a joint for the weekend.'

'Harvey's or Ensten's?'

'Well, I don't really know. I'd rather thought of the Co-op.'

'Excellent for pork.'

'To tell the truth, I've not bought a joint before. We've always had a chicken. But now he's got tired of chicken.'

Five months of love and chicken. . . .

'I'm afraid you've been spoiling him,' said Lois. 'Keep him on cold veal for a few weeks and he'll be thankful for chicken.'

'I hadn't thought of veal. Would veal be a good idea?'

'Here come your statement sheets. Now we can go and have some coffee and think about the veal.'

'Well, I must say, I'd be glad of it. Shopping gets me down.'

Tottering on stiletto heels and still a head shorter than Lois, the replacement preceded her from the bank, jostling the swinging doors with her two bulging, ill-assembled shopping bags. Lois took one from her. It was the bag whose handle Fenton, in a rush of husbandry, had mended with string. The string ground into her fingers—as fatal, as familiar, as ever.

The grey downs grew into lumps of sin to Guenevere in William Morris's poem, and as Fenton's wives sat drinking coffee the shopping bags humped on the third chair grew into lumps of sin to Lois. They were her bags, her burden; and she had cast them onto the shoulders of this hapless child and gone flourishing off, a free woman. It might be said, too, though she made less of it, that she had cast the child on Fenton's ageing shoulders and hung twenty-one consecutive frozen chicken round his neck . . . a clammy garland. Apparently it was impossible to commit the simplest act of selfishness, of self-defence even, without paining and inconveniencing others. Lost in these reflections, Lois forgot to keep the conversation going. It was Valerie who revived it. 'Where would one be without one's cup of coffee?'

For, considering how handicapped she was with middle age and morality, Fenton's other one had been putting up a creditable show of sophisticated broadmindedness, and deserved a helping hand—the more so since that sigh in the bank was now so clearly explainable as a sigh of regret for the days when she had a husband to cook for. Lois agreed that one would be quite lost without one's cup of coffee. 'And I always think it's such a mistake to put milk in it,' continued Valerie, who with presence of mind had refused milk, black coffee being more sophisticated. Two sophisticated women, keeping their poise on the rather skiddy surface of a serial husband, was how she saw the situation. For a while, she managed to keep conversation on a black-coffee level: foreign travel, television, the guitar. But you could see the poor thing's heart wasn't really in it; grieving for what could never again be hers, she just tagged along. Yes, she had been to Spain, but it was a long time ago. No, unfortunately, she had missed that programme. 'I never seem to have enough time. Do have another cake.' She seemed to have time enough now. The cake lay on her plate, the coffee cooled in her cup; still she sat brooding, and frowned as though she were calculating some odds, hatching some resolution. Could it be that she was going to turn nasty? All of a sudden, she looked up and exclaimed, 'I know. Oxtail.'

'I beg your pardon?'

'Oxtail. Instead of a joint. Come on.'

Well, if it made her happy . . .

It certainly did. A wife Fenton hadn't given her an idea of, a wife as animated and compelling as a scenic railway, swept Valerie to the butcher's, summoned old Mr. Ensten himself, made him produce a series of outlandish objects totally unlike Valerie's conception of what could be called a joint, chose out the most intimidating of the lot, stiff as a poker and a great deal longer, watched with a critical eye as he smote it into coilability, swept on to a greengrocer to buy carrots, garlic, celery and button mushrooms, then to a grocer's shop, bafflingly small, dusky and undisplaying, where she bought peppercorns, bay leaves and a jar of anchovies, finally to a wine merchant where she bought half a bottle of claret. Whirled on in this career, consulted and assenting over God knew what next, abandoning all thought of the rest of her shopping list, Valerie fell from gasps to giggles. Why peppercorns, when pepper could be got ready ground? Why anchovies, when there was no thought of fish? And garlic? Now it was claret.

'And a taxi, please.'

As though it were perfectly normal for wine merchants to supply taxis, the taxi was fetched. Valerie was put into it; the parcels and shopping bags were put in after her.

'Seventeen Windermere Gardens,' said Lois.

Once, escaping from the Secretarial College, Valerie and Olive Petty bought half-crown tickets for a Mystery Drive. The bus, thundering through a maze of small streets, had taken them past the Corporation Gas Works into the unknown. It had dived into woods, skirted past villages with spires and villages with towers, shown them

an obelisk on a hill-top, a reservoir, a bandstand, an Isola-
tion Hospital, a glimpse of the sea, a waterfall, a ruined
castle. Then, with a twirl through some unidentifiable
suburbs, it set them down by the War Memorial, a stone's
throw from the Secretarial College. Now it was to be the
same thing. The Mystery Shopping Excursion would end
at 17 Windermere Gardens. All that remained was to say
something calm and suitable.

'Such an unexpected pleasure to meet you. You've quite
changed the day for me.'

'But I'm coming, too. I'm coming to cook the oxtail. I
hope you don't mind.'

'Mind? My God, I'd be thankful! And more.'

The ring of sincerity transformed the poor girl's voice.
To say 'transfigured' would, however, be going too far.
Transformed it. Unmuzzled it.

No act of reparation, thought Lois, sitting in the taxi,
can be an exact fit. Circumstances are like seaweed: a
moment's exposure to the air, an hour's relegation to the
past tense, stiffens, warps, shrivels the one and the other.
The impulse to ease even a fraction of the burden she had
imposed on that very different Miss Valerie Fry of the
divorce proceedings—an impulse first felt in the bank as an
amused acknowledgement of a faint sense of guilt, which
at the word 'joint' had fleshed itself in the possibility of a
deed, and a compassion against which she had soon ceased
to struggle—for only someone in a state of utter dejection
could have eaten three of those appalling little cakes—
would fit neither the offence nor the moment. Probably
even the medium was ill chosen. She happened to like oxtail herself, but very likely the girl would have preferred
rolled ribs. Only one static element would resist the flux

of time: Fenton's planet-like, unconjectural course. The Borough Offices where he worked as an architect closed at midday on Saturday. The planet-like course then took him to lunch at the Red Lion, and then to a healthful swim in the public baths, and then to his club; and he would be home at six.

'I'm afraid, as I wasn't expecting you, there won't be more than bread and cheese,' said the voice, now back in its muzzle.

'Nothing I should like better. It will give us more time to cook in. When does Fenton usually get home?'

'Four, or thereabouts.'

Even Fenton wasn't the same. She glanced with admiration at the young person whose society was two hours more alluring than hers had been; then at her wristwatch.

'Well, if I don't dawdle over my bread and cheese, that should be long enough. At any rate, it should be well on its way by then.'

'By then? All that time to cook a tail? You *must* be fond of cooking!'

The tone of spontaneous contempt, thought Lois, was just what anyone trying to apply an act of reparation might expect, and therefore what she deserved.

The taxi turned down Windermere Terrace. Seeing the iteration of small houses, each carefully designed to be slightly at variance with the others, each with a small identical garage and small front gardens for demonstrations of individuality, Lois observed that in some of the gardens the ornamental shrubs had grown larger, in others had died. They entered the house.

'I should think it must feel a bit queer to you, coming back like this,' Valerie said.

'No. Rather homelike. What a pretty new wallpaper—new wallpapers, that is.' A pink wall with squiggles, a blue wall with stripes, a yellow wall with poodles, kiosks and the Eiffel Tower, a black wall with marbling. And did Fenton come home two hours earlier to gaze on these?

'I put them all on myself. And one with fishes in the bathroom. I expect you know your way to the bathroom?'

'I must not, will not, be censorious,' said Lois to herself. And Valerie, arranging ready-sliced bread and processed cheese for two, muttered to her four walls, when she was left alone with them, 'If she goes on being a condescending old ray of sunlight, I'll murder her.'

There was no time to expect that Lois knew her way to the kitchen. She was in it in a flash.

'I haven't really got around to decorating this yet. To tell the truth, I'm not all that struck on cooking.'

'Where do you keep the large stewpan?'

The large stewpan was traced to the cupboard under the stairs, where it held jam pots and spiders. But at some time it must have been used, for Lois had left it clean. The cooking knives were rusty, the wooden spoons had been used to stir paint. Moths and skewers were in every drawer she opened. Without a flutter of pity, of compunction, of remorse, of any of the feelings that should accompany an act of reparation as parsley and lemon accompany fried plaice or red-currant jelly jugged hare, Lois searched, and cleaned, and sharpened, and by quarter to three the oxtail was in the large stewpan, together with the garlic, carrots, bay leaves, peppercorns and celery.

'What about the mushrooms?' Valerie inquired. She had rubbed the mushrooms and did not intend to see them slighted.

'They go in later on.'

'Well, as you seem to be managing all right, perhaps I'll . . .'

'Yes, do.'

One of the things Fenton particularly liked about Valerie was her habit of awaiting him. A man likes to be awaited. At the end of a dull day's architecture, to find a wife quietly sitting, undistracted by any form of employment, not even reading a book, but just sitting and waiting and ready to look pleased is very agreeable. Today he happened to be forty minutes later than usual, a conversation with a man called Renshaw having delayed him. His expectations were forty minutes livelier, and as he closed the garage and walked towards his door he said to himself that there was really quite a dash of the Oriental in him. The discovery of this dash—he had not been aware of it till Valerie—had even reconciled him to the prospect of baked beans or scrambled eggs on cold toast, if such was the price of being awaited. Besides, he always had a good substantial lunch at the Red Lion. But today Valerie was awaiting him amid a most exhilarating smell of cooking. It would be gross to comment on it immediately: to mulct her of the caresses of reunion, to fob off her proper desire to hear what he had been doing all day. And though she did not comment on his unpunctuality, he was at pains to tell her of his unforeseen encounter with Renshaw—not the Renshaw who skated and had been instrumental in bringing them together but his cousin E. B. Renshaw; to recount what E. B. Renshaw had said and to give a brief account of his character, career and accomplishments as a slow bowler. Only then did he say, 'No need to ask what you've been doing. What a wonderful smell! What is it?'

'Oxtail.'

'Of course! Oxtail. I thought I knew it.'

'Do you like oxtail?'

'Immensely—when it's not out of the tin. I can smell that this isn't.'

'Oh, no!'

He snuffed again. Lois had added the mushrooms and the anchovies and was now administering claret.

'Delicious! What's in it?'

'All sorts of things. Button mushrooms.'

Her smile struck him as secretive—no wonder, with this talent up her sleeve. And all performed so casually, too, so unobtrusively; for there she sat, reposeful, not a hair out of place, none of the usual cook's airs of flurry and in-attention, not a single 'Just wait one moment' while he was relating his day and the meeting with E. B. Renshaw.

'When will it be ready?' he said with ardour.

'Not just yet. Do you like my nail varnish? It's new. I bought it today.'

'Very pretty. Do you think you ought to go and stir it?'

'Oh, no! She'll do all that.'

'She?' Had Valerie gone and got a cook? A cook from whom such odours proceeded would demand enormous wages, yet might almost be worth it. 'She? What she?'

'Your other wife. She's in there. She's been doing it all the afternoon.'

'Do you mean Lois?'

'Of course I mean Lois. You haven't any other wives, have you?'

This pertness when referring to his previous marriage was customary, and did not altogether displease. Now he didn't even notice it. He had a situation to grapple with, and the better to do so removed part of it off his knee.

'How did this happen?'

'We met at the bank—she'd gone there for some teapot or other. We couldn't sit there glaring at each other, so we began to talk.'

About him, of course. What confidences had been exchanged? What invidious——

'She told me you liked cold veal.'

A total misrepresentation. Lois had always been malicious, seizing on some casually expressed liking to throw in his teeth. 'What else did she say?'

'Nothing much. I had to do most of the talking. And before I knew where I was, she was wanting to come and cook you an oxtail. I couldn't very well stop her, could I? Of course I paid for it. The worst of it is, she was in such a rush to get here that I hadn't a chance to ask Strumpshaw about that sixpence, or to get the waistcoat buttons or the right liver salts or your China tea. She isn't what I'd call considerate.'

'I shall have to go and see her.'

He would have to open the kitchen door, take the full assault of that witching smell, see Lois cooking as of old—an unassimilable answer to prayer. For of course she mustn't come again, she mustn't go on doing this sort of thing; nor was he a man to be won back by fleshpots. Yet be knew himself moved. Poor Lois, making her way back almost like an animal, forgetting her jealousy, her prejudice, all the awful things she had said at the time of the divorce, trampling on convention and *amour-propre*, just to cook him a favourite dish. What had impelled her to do this? Remorse, loneliness, an instinctive longing to foster and nourish? For many years her feeling for him had been almost wholly maternal—which made her insistence on the divorce even more uncalled-for. What had set it off? Seeing the teapot, perhaps. They had both been fond of the teapot. It was Georgian.

Or was it all a deliberate scheme to lure him back?

He sprang to his feet, straightened his waistcoat, left the sitting room, entered the kitchen. It was empty. She had gone. Tied to the handle of the stewpan was a visiting card, on the back of which she had written: 'This will be ready by seven. It should simmer till then. *Don't let it boil.*'

# THEIR QUIET LIVES

THE window was shut. Outside was an April sky, tufted with small white clouds, and a semi-rustic landscape dotted with red-roofed new bungalows whose television masts controverted the anarchy of some old apple trees, a sufficient number of which had been preserved to justify the title of The Orchard Estate.

Once again, Mrs. Drew consulted her watch. The watch was attached to her bosom by a matching enamel brooch; to turn its face upwards and bend her own over it involved a certain degree of effort, and made her grunt. But though there was a clock on the mantelshelf, she preferred to consult her watch. For one thing, it had sentimental value; her husband had given it to her as a honeymoon present, fifty years earlier. For another, she could trust it. Audrey had more than once forgotten to wind the clock.

Three minutes to eleven. No doubt her Bovril would be late. Dr. Rice Thompson had said repeatedly that with a digestion like hers regularity was everything. But one does not expect too much. One has learned not to. Two minutes to eleven. At eleven precisely, the door burst open. Audrey came in with her stumping tread.

'Mother! Mother! Did you hear? The cuckoo?'

'What, dear?'

'The cuckoo. The first cuckoo.'

'What, dear? Has something gone wrong?'

There was nothing wrong with the tray, that she could

see. The toast was nicely browned, the pepper caster had been remembered. So why did not Audrey put it down?

'The first cuckoo, Mother. Spring has come.'

'Who has come? I wish you'd tell me. I can stand up to bad news better than suspense. And do put that tray down. If you aren't careful, you'll slop it.'

Audrey put down the tray and slopped it as she did so.

'The cuckoo, Mother.'

'Oh. The cuckoo. . . . I can't hear it.'

'No. It's left off.'

So much confusion and nonsense about a bird that came year after year and more or less at the same date. But the Bovril was delicious. It swept down her, a reviving tide, and renewed her interest in life.

'Has the paper come?'

'Not yet.'

'Tchah! It's always late now. Why is it always late?'

'Because it comes with the milk.'

'But it has always come with the milk.'

'Yes. But now there are all these new houses, you see, all having milk, so the milkman takes longer to get to us.'

'I don't see at all.'

For the last eighteen months this conversation about the newspaper and the milk had taken place daily.

But everything, thought Audrey, is more or less daily. Daily, her brother Donald caught the 8.5 in order to reach his office at 9 with a few minutes in hand to feed the city pigeons. Daily at 10.50 she squared the crust off two slices of bread and put them in the electric toaster to accompany the eleven-o'clock Bovril. Daily at 2.30 she arranged her mother on the sofa for an afternoon sleep and had an hour or so to herself. Daily at 5.55 the bell of St. Botolph's sounded its twenty strokes and she slipped off to Evensong. Nightly at 10.30, having settled Mother in bed and emptied the sink basket, she noted down the day's expenses, wrote in her diary and read the Psalms for the day. The milkman, the postman, the baker, the B.B.C. announcers —all rolled round in a diurnal course along with Wordsworth's Lucy; though Lucy rolled unconsciously, being dead.

Luncheon, too, was daily; and today it involved both mincing and sieving, so she would have to set about it immediately. As she was leaving the room, her mother said, 'By the way, you'll have to order extra milk if . . .' There she stopped.

'If what, Mother?'

'If you make a milk pudding.'

Poor Mother! It was sad to see her trying to assert her former hold on life.

'Yes, Mother. I'll remember.'

Hearing the door close, Mrs. Drew chuckled. Good Lord, that had been a near thing! It was no part of her plan to mention Betty Sullivan until she was sure of her. Fortunately, she had kept her head, and turned it off with a pudding.

The milkman came in his diurnal course, and Audrey carried in *The Daily Telegraph*. Mother turned with avidity to the Deaths. When other helpers fail and comforts flee, when the senses decay and the mind moves in a narrower and narrower circle, when the grass hopper is a burden and the postman brings no letters, and even the Royal Family is no longer quite what it was, an obituary column stands fast. On days when it failed to record the death of someone Mother knew, it would almost certainly provide a name familiar to her, and this would be dwelt on with speculation and gathering confidence.

Today the name was Polson.

'Polson. Gertrude Polson. Pepper, please; you never put in enough pepper nowadays. I met her at Malvern. We were staying in one hotel and she was staying in another, and we met at the lending library. Such a charming woman, and I'm almost sure her name was Gertrude. She looked frail even then, though. Gertrude Polson, in her eighty-seventh year. I don't suppose you remember her.'

'I don't think I do.'

'No, you wouldn't. We were at Malvern in 1917, when you were three. There was a Mr. Poison, too—he etched or something. But the announcement doesn't mention him, it just says that she died peacefully in a nursing home at Castle Bromwich. I expect there was a divorce.'

In some ways, Mother's presumptive deaths were even better than her valid ones. They afforded her more scope. But though Mrs. Polson brightened lunch, tea was clouded by the usual disappointment. 'Where are the letters? Hasn't the post come?'

'Yes, it's come. But there were no letters for you this afternoon.'

'No letters? Are you sure? Did you look carefully?'

'Yes, Mother. Two for Donald, and a circular for me. Nothing else.'

'Are you sure there wasn't a letter for me? With a Devon postmark?'

'Were you expecting a letter from Devonshire?'

Mrs. Drew looked at her daughter as though seeing her steadily and whole, and said, 'Fool!'

At 5.55 the bell of St. Botolph's rang for Evensong. Audrey went to church through an exquisite evening, the evening of the day when she had heard the first cuckoo; and prayed to be made perfect in patience. Mrs. Drew continued to extort patience till her bedtime.

'What's wrong with Mother?' Donald inquired when Audrey came downstairs to empty the sink basket. 'Has anything upset her?'

'She didn't get some letter she was expecting—from Devonshire. I do wish she could get more letters, poor old thing!'

'Perhaps she'll have one tomorrow.'

The expected letter, addressed in a curly, dashing hand and post-marked Exeter, was in the morning post. Mrs. Drew tore it open, read it with obvious satisfaction, replaced it in the envelope and said she would have a poached egg for her breakfast. It was after she had drunk her eleven-o'clock Bovril that she remarked, 'There's not much on a duck, so I think you had better order a couple. Why are you looking at me like that? Didn't you hear me? I said, order a couple of ducks.'

'But ducks are still very expensive, Mother. It's only April, you know. And one duck is more than enough for three.'

'Four.'

'Four ducks?'

'No! Two ducks. Four people. Betty Sullivan's coming. I suppose you can remember *her*, at least.'

'Oh yes. She was your great friend when you were a girl, wasn't she? And married a lawyer. What day is she coming?'

'The day after tomorrow.'

'How nice! You will enjoy seeing her again. For lunch?'
'To stay.'
'Over the weekend? I'll get the spare room ready.'
'For a couple of months.'
'Months, Mother?'
'Months, Audrey. Or longer, if she likes. And I wish you'd go and have your ears syringed. I'm not strong enough to have to say everything twice over. And don't bother about the spare room. She'll be bringing a lot of luggage with her—she's giving up the lodgings she moved into after Gerald Sullivan died and that odious daughter-in-law of hers insisted that they'd inherited the house and moved into it with a pack of children. It can't possibly all get into the spare room, so she will have to have your room and you can have the spare room. Has the paper come?'

'Not yet. It comes with the milk, you know.'
'That's no reason for it to be late.'
'It isn't late, Mother. It comes later, that's all. But, Mother, about Mrs. Sullivan . . .'
'Well?' Mrs. Drew's neck crimsoned.
'I didn't know she was a widow,' said Audrey hastily. For though Mother's blood pressure would sooner or later carry her off—whereby everything would be greatly simplified—Audrey did not wish to bring on a stroke in order to avert Mrs. Sullivan. That must be Donald's part. A son has more authority. And it was only fair that Donald should undertake Mother occasionally, instead of talking about Quietism and leaving everything to her. After a few words about Mrs. Sullivan's widowhood (which, bursting on Mrs. Drew through the column of Deaths, had called forth a letter of condolence, and a renewal of former intimacy),

Audrey said no more and spent the afternoon tidying the spare room.

Nuns, she recalled, are contented with their narrow cells. Considering the spare room in this light she felt that with a transference of pillows and a removal of all the pictures and ornaments she might be quite happy in it. For one thing, it would make a change; for another, it was at the other end of the passage from Mother; for yet another, it was definitely more cellular, and so might be thought of as a sort of ante-cell to the little whitewashed room under a beehive roof that awaited her in South Africa. 'We will take you at any moment,' Sister Monica had said. 'Just send a cable and get a plane.'

Chief among the things which Mrs. Drew's blood pressure would ultimately simplify was the matter of her children's religious vocations. Audrey's was the more compact. She was an oblate of an Anglican sisterhood, and at a retreat she had met Sister Monica, on leave from the daughter house in Africa. By the end of the retreat Audrey felt sure of her vocation and Sister Monica had provisionally accepted her. It was only a question, as the nun remarked, of keeping her passport up to date and waiting on the Lord. While Audrey waited on the Lord, Donald was going through more complicated spiritual adjustments. There were times when he even thought of becoming a Buddhist. Just now he felt almost certain that he would become a Roman Catholic and enter a contemplative order. But all this had to be kept from Mother, who prided herself on despising all forms of religion impartially—though if she were to discover Donald's present way of thinking she would be ready to shed the last drop of his blood for the Protestant faith.

Instead of coming straight back from Evensong Audrey intercepted Donald at the station and told him about Betty Sullivan. He pooh-poohed it, with every sign of alarm. 'I shan't say a word about it,' he declared, 'unless Mother does.' And while Audrey was getting dinner he retired to the tool shed and oiled the lawnmower.

The lawnmower had been put away dirty—he would not say by whom—so he had to clean it, too. He could not but think it unfair that he, working all day in the office, should find himself expected to deal with poor Mother's vagaries the moment he got back. That was a daughter's part. And it was all very well for Audrey to secrete a vocation to be a nun in Africa, but here and now her vocation was to be a daughter in Middlesex.

At 7.30, Mother sat down at the head of the table, made sure that the pepper caster was within reach, and said, 'Audrey, have you remembered to order those ducks?'

Audrey glanced meaningly at Donald, who said, 'Duck? Are we going to have roast duck? How delightful!'

'No, Mother. We can't afford them. I asked, and they are twenty-five shillings each. Isn't it wicked?'

Disregarding the moral issue Mother said, 'And may I ask who pays for the food in this house? You haven't got that power of attorney yet, you know.'

Donald raising his voice remarked, 'Audrey, this is very nice soup.'

Audrey's silence and Mother's ominous sotto-voce 'Not yet, not yet, not yet!' drove him to speak again.

'By the way, Mother, returning to the duck, do you particularly want a duck? I might be able to find a cheaper one in London.'

'I never said I wanted a duck. I want two ducks. I wish

you and Audrey would listen to me occasionally, and not wink at each other. You're as bad as Betty Sullivan.'

'Who is Betty Sullivan?' 'Does Mrs. Sullivan wink?' Donald and Audrey spoke simultaneously.

'Of course she winks. She's always winked. But in her case, it's nervous. It only comes on when she's angry. And it's quite uncontrollable; she can't be blamed for it. Not like you two, winking at each other all through meals, like semaphores.'

Donald started. Audrey had kicked him sharply on the ankle. 'We seem to have lost sight of the duck,' he began. 'As I said, if you want a duck, I might be able to——'

'I said nothing of the sort. I said I wanted two ducks. And I mean to have them. I don't call five shillings a great deal for a duck.'

'Twenty-five shillings!' shouted Donald, roused at last.

'Twenty-five shillings, if you like,' said his mother airily. 'Are we going to have anything besides soup, Audrey?'

Donald could be relied upon to put up a pretty good fight when money was concerned so Audrey took her time over dishing up the braised lamb. Their voices grew increasingly louder, increasingly alike. Donald was certainly engaged; she would leave him to it for a little longer. In the event, she left him too long. When she took in the lamb, he was saying, 'Well, I wash my hands of it.' The lamb was eaten in silence. During the pudding there was a little conversation about the cuckoo.

Apparently Donald had also washed his hands of the washing up, which he ordinarily helped in. When Audrey returned to the sitting room he had turned on the wireless and was listening to a talk about the thraldom of writers behind the Iron Curtain. Mother's neck was no longer crimson. Her hooked nose, which in moments of wrath asserted itself as it would when she lay dead, had sunk back into the mass of her face and she looked as composed as a sea anemone digestively sealed on its prey. Excerpts from *The Merry Widow* followed the thraldom of Soviet writers. Donald continued to listen. When she had settled Mother in bed, he was having a bath. She waited for him to come out, and pounced.

'Well, Donald. So you've decided to give in.'

'No. Not exactly. But I think we should give way. Not to the ducks, of course. That's palpably absurd, and you must get round it. But give way about this Sullivan person. After all, she is our mother.'

'You mean, Mother is.'

Donald for a moment looked exactly as Mother had done before ejaculating 'Fool!'

'As you say, Audrey, she is our mother. Her life is monotonous, she lives in the past, she has never realized that her money is only worth half what it was twenty years ago. She has set her heart on seeing Mrs. Sullivan. Anyhow, it won't be for long. They are bound to quarrel. Mother quarrels with everyone after a week. Are we to grudge her this little pleasure?'

Stalking down the passage in his bare feet and his plaid dressing gown, he looked positively apostolic. Even in the nursery she had made it her business to shelter her little brother. The little brother was now going bald. The sheltering process had gone on too long.

Two days later, and with a great quantity of small pieces of luggage, Betty Sullivan arrived.

'Betty!'

Poppy!'

'After all these years!'

'But I'd know you anywhere!'

They continued to exclaim. Audrey continued to carry the small pieces of luggage upstairs. One of them was so unexpectedly heavy that she exclaimed, too. Mrs. Sullivan turned round. 'And is this your Audrey?'

'How do you do.'

'Why, you might be your great-aunt! Poppy, isn't she exactly like your Aunt Ada? Don't bother with that parcel, dear. It can stay. Poppy! You'll never guess what I've brought. All my old snapshot albums.'

Though Mrs. Sullivan's face was more ravaged than Mother's she had kept some modicum of her waist and seemed the younger of the two. In fact, as Audrey realized when called on to look at a snapshot of two pigtailed girls in skirts down to their ankles, Poppy and Betty were exact contemporaries. Now they sat on the sofa with the albums, elatedly identifying people with names like Bertie and Nina.

Ducks require basting, so Audrey had to forgo Even song. The oven door was open and the basting in process when Donald looked in.

'What's she like? She seems to talk a—— You don't mean to say you bought those ducks?'

'I gave way, Donald. After all, she is our mother.'

'Well, I suppose it's too late now. But I wish you hadn't.'

Having left the kitchen, Donald speedily returned. 'Audrey! What's this frightful smell all over the house?'

'I expect it's Mrs. Sullivan's scent.'

'Good God! But it's everywhere.'

'She's been everywhere. Mother's been showing her

round. She put some on Mother, too. I t'scalled *Méfie-toi.*'

While Poppy and Betty continued to evoke the past—to recall hockey matches, blue voile, fox terriers, confirmation classes, the Bishop's boots; while Mother, animated by these feasts of memory, grew increasingly demanding and autocratic and Audrey increasingly jaded and fatalistic, Donald was being driven frantic by *Méfie-toi.* He bought aerosols, he sprayed the bathroom with disinfectant, he soaked his handkerchief in citronella and pressed it convulsively to his nose whenever Mrs. Sullivan came near him. He pressed it so convulsively that after a few days his nose became inflamed. Mrs. Sullivan, calling him her poor boy, insisted on applying a cooling lotion—one of the *Méfie-toi* series. Trying to remove the stink from his nostrils with carbolic soap and a nailbrush, Donald rubbed himself raw. This wasn't so obsessive in the train, for there he could hold up his newspaper. But one cannot walk through the streets of London with a newspaper before one's face, and it seemed to him that people were either looking at his nose or avoiding looking at it. Then Holiday, with whom he lunched on Tuesdays, said to him, 'You ought to take care of that nose, Drew.' The same evening, when he turned to Audrey for sympathy, she blinked at him as though he were a very long way off and remarked that she had a pain in her stomach. Donald replied that he was sorry to hear it—Audrey had expressed no sorrow about his nose—and added that it was probably colic, arising from the richness of the food since Mrs. Sullivan had been with them. As Audrey did the cooking, the remedy was in her own hands.

Two evenings later Audrey fell off her chair during

dinner and lay writhing on the floor. When they tried to pull her up she screamed. Dr. Rice Thompson was sent for, and she was taken to hospital in an ambulance and operated on for acute appendicitis.

When Audrey came round from the anaesthetic and saw only strange faces bending over her she gave a sigh of relief and burrowed back into unconsciousness. Some time later—how much later she did not know or care—she opened her eyes and there was Donald. A voice from somewhere said, 'Not more than five minutes, Mr. Drew.' Donald sat down and gazed at a kidney basin.

'How are you all getting on?' she asked.

'Splendidly!'

'Oh.' She felt a vague relief and also a vague surprise. 'I'm so glad.'

'You needn't worry about us. Betty got Hannah.'

Hanna. Hanna in the wilderness. Probably some kind of patent food. Well, if it satisfied them . . .. Then her conscience woke up and told her that poor Donald was putting a brave face on it. 'What is——'

At the same moment Donald continued, 'Hannah is her old servant. Betty telegraphed and Hannah came by the next train, and does everything. I must say, Betty has been very helpful. I've never eaten better pastry. And Betty's arranged with her to stay on for a week after you're back to ease you in.'

'Oh. Where does she sleep, this Hannah?'

'She's sleeping out. She fixed it up with the greengrocer. He's a Wesleyan, too. They're thick as thieves, and he lets her have asparagus for next to nothing. I could never be a Wesleyan myself—but there's something rather beautiful in such a simple outlook.'

No one is wholly pleased at learning that he has been replaced by someone who does as well or better. Only by exerting her lower nature, by reflecting on such domestic offices as cleaning round the bathroom taps and washing the milk bottles, was Audrey able to repose on the thought that Betty Sullivan's Hannah, lodging at Powell's and coming in to get Donald's breakfast, would be there when she got home.

Betty Sullivan arrived in a hired car to fetch Audrey away and throughout the drive was everything that was kind and everything that was hospitable. 'I want you to feel as free as if you were staying in a hotel,' she insisted. 'A nice restful little hotel, where you've only got to ring a bell. I've put one of your mother's bells in your room. It's absurd for her to have five hand bells, even if they do have associations. So you've got the one that Madge Massingham-Maple gave her as a wedding present. She never really cared for poor old Madge.'

'How is Mother?'

'In wonderful form. Top-hole. Fit as a flea.'

Audrey had scarcely greeted her mother before she was being put to bed. Tea, with homemade cake, was brought in by Hannah. It was a Saturday, and presently she heard Donald mowing the lawn. The millennium could not last. The bills would be appalling. Mother looked dangerously red. Betty had somehow got at the best tea service and Hannah would undoubtedly break it. Sooner or later, there would be the devil to pay, and *Méfie-toi* would hang about the house for months. Meanwhile she would make the most of this unexpected sojourn in a nice restful little home where she had only to ring Madge Massingham-Maple's bell.

But nothing whatever went wrong. Hannah was an

excellent manager as well as an admirable cook and seemed prepared to stay on indefinitely. So, of course, did Betty Sullivan, but this was not altogether a matter for regret. Not only was Betty an adjunct to Hannah; not only was she contributing, and pretty handsomely, to the household expenses; but since her arrival Mother had become a changed being, a being with an interest in life. They talked untiringly about their girlhood—about the winters when they went skating, the summers when they went boating, the period when they were so very pious, the period when they were pious no longer and sent a valentine to the curate: the curate blushed, a crack ran out like a pistol shot and Hector Gillespie went through the ice, the fox terriers fought under old Mrs. Bulliver's chair, the laundry ruined the blue voile, the dentist cut his throat in Centry Wood, Claude Hopkins came back from Cambridge with a motor-car and drove it at thirty miles an hour with flames shooting out behind, Addie Carew was married with a wasp under her veil. From time to time, they pursued themselves into their later years—into marriage, maternity, butter coupons, the influenza epidemic, the disappearance of washstands, poor Lucy Latrobe who took to drink, Mr. Drew going out for an evening paper and being brought back dead, Addie's pretty granddaughter rushing from one divorce to the next. But over these years the conversation did not flow so serenely. There were awkward passages where Betty boasted, where Poppy criticized. So presently they travelled back to the days of their youth, and told the same stories over again and laughed with inexhaustible delight at the same misfortunes. The windows stood open, summer curtains frisked in the breeze and Mother felt so well that she and Betty made several excursions to London, to choose new chair covers, to lunch at little places in Soho.

Audrey and Donald wallowed in unprincipled peacefulness—to Audrey, at any rate, it seemed unprincipled, for she was ill-acquainted with pleasures not snatched from the jaws of duty.

'Do you know what I've been thinking?' said Donald. They were in the garden, collecting slugs by twilight. From the kitchen came the sound of Hannah washing up, from the sitting room the story of Hector Gillespie going through the ice.

'No, what?' she said apprehensively.

'That now's your time.'

'Now's my time?'

'Now's your time. To get away. If you went to Africa now, Mother would scarcely notice it. Listen to her! She's completely happy, living in the past. And if you go, Betty will certainly stay on. It would be just the excuse she needs for staying here, in reach of London.'

'But if now's my time, isn't it your time, too?'

'It's not so urgent for me. And not such plain sailing.'

'You're thinking Mother couldn't live without you—without your salary?'

'I'm thinking nothing of the sort,' he said with acerbity. 'Betty's very well off. You've only to look at her—you've only to smell her to know that. Besides, I happen to know.'

'But how? Did she tell you?'

He scooped up another slug with his teaspoon and dropped it into the jar of salt water.

'As a matter of fact, I sent Lorna—my secretary—to the Probate Office to have a look at Gerald's will.'

A voice from indoors exclaimed, 'Betty, you've got that

wrong again! You always get it wrong. Bertie Gillespie was dancing with me—not with Mabel.'

'Very well, very well. Have it your own way, dear.'

Their tones made it apparent that Betty Sullivan was winking, that Mother's neck was crimsoning. From time to time, they had these girlish tiffs.

'But, Donald—I shall have to tell her.'

'You can tell her that Sister Monica has invited you to go there for a month, to convalesce.'

Such resourcefulness, such solicitude for her vocation, such readiness to stand aside and let her get away. . . . Poor Donald! How she had misjudged him! For years she had thought him selfish. Yet now he stood beside her, a strong brotherly presence, prepared to suffer in her stead—not only Mother, either; for he suffered as much as ever from *Méfie-toi*, which was why he was sharing the slug hunting, and why he often did not come home till the last train, making a supper of sandwiches on the Embankment or in some quiet city churchyard in order to avoid it. For years, Audrey had been misjudging Donald; and within half an hour she was misjudging him again. The more she thought of it, the more penetrating became her impression that Donald had something up his sleeve and was trying to get rid of her.

Feeling in some vague way menaced, she took refuge in a precautionary inertia. The way of escape stood open—at least, Donald assured her it did. Mother needed her no longer, infinitely preferring Betty's company and Hannah's cooking. Nothing tied her to a home where, since she slept in its spare room, she was already in part a stranger. She had not even to buy an outfit, for when she arrived at the convent she would put on her novice's habit. Inoculations, topee, sunglasses—everything would be provided. She had only to make up her mind. But instead of letting itself be made up, her mind drifted away to suppositions and excuses. Was she well enough? Had Sister Monica really meant it? Oughtn't she to wait till Mother died? Was she sure of her vocation? What was Donald really up to? And when Donald inquired if she had written to the convent, if she had found out about flights, she put him off with adhesions, old letters that must be sorted and disposed of, a bank manager that must be visited.

'I warn you, Audrey. Time is getting short.'

'What do you mean? Why is it any shorter than it was last week?'

'It is a week shorter. Didn't you hear Mother yesterday evening?'

'Yesterday evening? Yes, they did have rather a tiff, but they often have tiffs. And then they make it up again.'

'Before very long, they'll have a tiff and not make it up again. Mark my words, Audrey. Time is getting short. Don't say I didn't warn you.'

These words provoked the inevitable reaction. Audrey laughed in an elder-sisterly way and said that if Donald had seen as much of Mother as she had done, he wouldn't think much of yesterday evening. Donald, his nose standing out like Mother's at its most embattled, said he would say no more, and added that he would be away for the weekend.

The sight of Donald going away with a little bag, to mind his own business instead of hers, restored Audrey's confidence in her purpose. She checked her passport and sent a cable to Sister Monica; on Monday she would go up to London and book her flight. All this took no time at all, and she spent the afternoon tearing up old diaries and parcelling clothes to be sent to the Church Army. Walking to Evensong through a downpour of thundery rain, she seemed to be moving under an invisible umbrella that sheltered her from alternatives and second thoughts far more efficiently than the visible umbrella, which had holes in it, sheltered her from the downpour. In the same heavenly frame of mind she walked home and entered the house.

The sound of violent altercation came from the sitting room.

'I tell you, you've got it wrong. You've been singing it wrong ever since I first knew you.'

'Well, that's a lie, anyhow. You first knew me when we were at the kindergarten—and they hadn't been published then. We're not so young as you try to make out, Betty.'

'I didn't know you at the kindergarten—not to call it knowing. I merely disliked you, because you sat on your hair and never left off saying so.'

'I can sit on it to this day.'

'Well, suppose you can? Is that the be-all and end-all of existence? But we're not talking about your hair, Poppy. We're talking about the Indian Love Lyrics. And I tell you again, you get it wrong. It goes like this: "Less, pom-pom-pom, than the dust, pom-pom-pom, be-Neath, pom-pom, thy chariot Whee-heel." The way you sing it, it sounds like a hymn.'

'The way you sing it, it sounds like a railway accident.'

Terrified of what she might overhear next, Audrey crept away. Her umbrella was still in her hand. She opened the kitchen door. 'Hannah. May I leave my umbrella to drip in the sink?'

Hannah sat at the table, shelling peas. 'Leave it where you like, Miss Drew. I don't know what Mr. Powell thinks he's doing, calling these fresh garden peas. Maggots in every pod! I've got more than a mind to throw the whole lot back in his face.'

Audrey crept away from the kitchen. She went up to the spare room, fell on her knees among the tidy confident parcels for the Church Army, and prayed with her hands over her ears. During dinner she tried so slavishly to speak peace to Mother and Betty that they unitedly bit her head off. Well, if it united them. . . .

For the time being, it did. Sunday might almost have been called a day of rest, if it had not been for Hannah, who slammed in and out looking harried and injured, and when offered praises of a gooseberry tart replied ominously that no one could say that she hadn't always tried to give satisfaction. The next day, as is usual after Sunday, was Monday. Audrey had dedicated Monday to seeing her bank manager and booking her passage. But she did neither, for in the course of discussing whether their next outing should be to Windsor or Box Hill Mother became so curt and Betty so bridling that she was afraid to leave them alone together. All day she longed, as she had never thought it possible to long, for Donald's return; and when she saw him at the gate, she rushed out and drew him into the tool shed.

'Donald! It's too awful! You were quite right, I feel it will break up at any moment, and Betty and Hannah will go off in a huff—for Hannah's furious, too, and has turned against Powell. And now we shall never get away.'

'You're leaving on Wednesday—the day after to-morrow.'

'The day after tomorrow?'

'I knew you'd put off doing anything, so I fixed it all up

this morning. I couldn't get a direct flight, so you'll have to change at Amsterdam, and spend a night in Athens, and go on from there by a plane that carries freight and one or two passengers. But you'll find it all perfectly easy and straightforward.'

'The day after tomorrow!'

'You can make some excuse—the dentist or something —and travel up with me on the 8.5. And I'll see you off. So all you've got to do now is to pay me for your tickets and behave as if nothing were up.'

'And tell Mother.'

'I will tell Mother.'

'*You* will tell Mother? Donald, do you mean it?'

'Certainly. I shall tell her that evening, when I get back. I've been thinking it out. It will be far better to tell her then, when it's all past praying for. The shock will draw them together.'

She stared at him. In the dusk of the tool shed his face was smug and moon-like—as the face of some all-sufficing, all-managing, miraculously intervening angel would naturally be.

'I'm hungry,' he said. 'Let's go in and hurry up Hannah. And we'll have a bottle of Graves. I feel like celebrating.'

On Wednesday, after a day during which her efforts to exercise a calming influence brought down on her a lecture from Betty about showing more consideration for Poppy's blood pressure and a considered critique from Mother wherein her stupidity, her virginity, her grovellings at St. Botolph's, her lifelong failure to exhibit a spark of initiative and her parsimony over buying new toothbrushes were severally laid forth and enlarged on; after a night of being alternately devoured by conscience and by a conviction that one or other of those planes would crash, Audrey caught the 8.5 with Donald. He accompanied her to the airport, assuring her from time to time that once she was on the plane everything would be easy and from time to time glancing covertly at his watch. At the airport they had twenty minutes to wait. Donald ordered coffee. His conversation was repetitive, and he seemed to have something on his mind. Remembering what lay before him, Audrey thought this was only reasonable. They sat at a little table and round them other people sat at other little tables, and it was as though this were some unnaturally hospitable out-patients' department. Another group of doomed travellers, these doomed to perish on a flight to Brussels, was summoned and rose up. The doors opened on a roar of propellers, and closed behind them. Swallowing with terror, Audrey said, 'Donald, I shall pray for you this evening. When will you do it? Before dinner or after?'

'Do it? Oh, tell Mother, you mean. As soon as I get back. After all, I shall have to explain why you're not with me.'

'About quarter to seven.'

'Or thereabouts. They should be back from their outing by then.'

'I'm afraid she will be very angry.'

'Yes. That's what I'm counting on.'

The surmise that Donald had something up his sleeve darted back and transfixed her. 'Counting on?'

'Yes. You see, I shall be killing two birds with one stone. First I shall tell her about you going off to Africa. Then about my marriage.'

'Donald! Are you going to marry?'

'I am married. I married Lorna—my secretary—ten

days ago. And I've been waiting to get you safe off to Africa so that I can begin with that, and draw the worst of her fire. As a matter of fact, I mean to say that you promised to break the news to her at the weekend while I was away—and that you forgot to. It can't hurt you, you'll be safe out of it. And it may make a great difference to me.'

'Then if there's a crash and I'm killed, it will serve me right!' The words burst from her. It was as if her fear, raw and bleeding, had been torn out and lay on the table between the coffee cups. 'Donald, I must go back! I can't think why I gave in to you. How could I do such a thing? Leave Mother without a word? Why, it might kill her. Oh, poor Mother! And you wouldn't have the slightest idea what to do for her. You've never even seen her in one of her attacks.'

'Hannah will be there.'

'I must have been mad to think of it. And just to make things easier for you—for that's all it amounts to. Really, Donald, for cold-blooded selfishness . . . Why are you looking at me like that?' He continued to look at her. 'No, I must go back. I must be there when you tell her about your being married. Besides, if I'm there, you won't have to tell her. You'll be able to leave everything to me. As usual!'

Donald appeared to be considering this. Then he shook his head. 'No, Audrey. I know what I'm about, and it will be far better if you are out of the way. For years, you've been getting on Mother's nerves——'

'Oh!'

'—and she's been getting on yours. Look at the state you're in now, working yourself up, as if planes crashed

every time someone who's left a mother is on board. Besides, everyone with a vocation goes through something
of this sort. Think of St. Chantal, walking over her son's
body. Concentrate on your vocation, Audrey. They're ex
pecting you. The tickets are bought. You can post a letter
to Mother from Amsterdam, if you want to—in fact, I
think you should. It's all perfectly straightforward, and by
this evening . . .'

'Attention, please,' said the impartially summoning
voice.

'Oh, poor Mother, poor Mother!'

'Audrey! Pull yourself together. People are beginning
to look at us.'

That did the trick. Appearing only moderately distraught, Audrey let herself be put on the plane, sank into
an embracing seat, fastened her belt and began to read the
advertisements. As the plane taxied interminably along the
runway, everything became a certainty. A few minutes of
remorse; then an explosion in which her cry for forgiveness would be lost. The plane rose. She looked down on
reeling buildings, roofs fleeing like frightened sheep, a surprising quantity of trees. A moment later, she forgot everything in the realization that she was going to be sick.

In Athens a cable was handed to her: 'MOTHER DIED
CLIMBING BOX HILL.'

# TOTAL LOSS

WHEN Charlotte woke, it was raining. Rain hid the view of the downs and blurred the neat row of trees and the neat row of houses opposite which the trees had been planted to screen. This was the third wet morning since her birthday a week ago. There would be rain all through the holidays, just like last year. On her birthday, Charlotte was ten. 'Now you are in double figures,' said Professor Bayer. 'And you will stay in them till you are a hundred years old. Think of that, my Lottchen.' 'Yes, think of that,' said Mother. Charlotte could see that Mother did not really wish to think of it. She was being polite, because Professer Bayer was a very important person at the Research Station, so it was a real honour that he should like Father and come to the house to borrow *The New Statesman.*

Charlotte's cat Moodie was awake already. He lay on the chair in the corner, on top of her clothes, and was staring at her with a thirsty expression. She jumped out of bed, went to the kitchen, breaking into its early morning tidiness and seclusion, and came back with a saucer of milk. 'Look, Moodie! Nice milk.' He would not drink, though he still had that thirsty expression. 'You silly old Moodles, you don't know what you want,' she said, kneeling before the chair with the saucer in her hand. Moodie had come as a wedding present to Mother. His birthday was unknown, but he was certainly two years older than Charlotte. Ever since she could remember, there had been Moodie, and Moodie had been hers—to be slept on, talked to, hauled about, wheeled in a doll's perambulator, read aloud to, confided in, wept on, trodden on, loved and taken for granted. He stared at her, ignoring the milk, and forgetting the milk she stared back, fascinated as ever by the way the fur grew on his nose, the mysterious smooth conflict between two currents of growth. At last she put down the saucer, seized him in her arms and got back into bed. 'We understand each other, don't we?' she said, curling his tail round his flank. 'Don't we, Moodie?' He trod with his front paws, purring under his breath, and relaxed, his head on her breast. But at the smell of his bad teeth she turned her face away, pretending it was to look out of the window. 'It's raining, Moodie. It's going to be another horrible wet day. You mustn't be a silly cat, sitting in the garden and getting wet through, like you did on Tuesday.' He was still purring when she fell asleep, though when her mother came to wake her he had gone. Sure enough, when she looked for him after breakfast he was sitting hunched and motionless on the lawn, his grey fur silvered with moisture and fluffed out like a coat of eiderdown. She picked him up, and the bloom vanished; the eiderdown coat, suddenly dark and lank, clung to his bony haunches. 'Mother, I'm going to put Moodie in the airing cupboard.'

'Yes, do, my pet. That's the best plan! But hurry, because Mr. and Mrs. Flaxman will be here to fetch you at any moment. They've just rung up. They want you to spend the day with them.'

'And see the horses?'

The cat in the child's arms broke into a purr, as though her thrill of pleasure communicated itself to him. Though of course it was really the warmth of the kitchen, thought Meg.

'Yes, the horses. And the bantams. And the lovely old toy theatre that belonged to Mrs. Flaxman's grandmother. You'll love it. It's an absolutely storybook house.'

'Shall I wear my new mac?'

'Yes. But hurry, Charlotte. Put Moodie in the airing cupboard, and wash your hands. I'll be up in a moment to brush your hair.'

She had made one false step. The Flaxmans lived twenty miles away, and if they had just rung up they could not be arriving immediately. Luckily Charlotte, though brought up to use her reason, was not a very deductive child; the discrepancy between the prompt arriving of the Flaxmans and the long drive back to Hood House was not likely to catch her attention. But perhaps a private word to Adela Flaxman—just to be on the safe side.

'Mother! Mother!'

At the threatening woe of the cry, Meg left everything and ran.

'Mother! There's a button off.'

The Flaxmans arrived, both talking at once, and saying what a horrible day it was, and Oh, the wretched farmers, who would be a farmer? in loud gay voices. Mrs. Flaxman was Mother's particular friend, but today Mother didn't seem to like her so much, and was laughing obligingly, just as she did with Professor Bayer. As Charlotte stood on the outskirts of this conversation she began to feel less sure of a happy successful day out. She would be treated like a child and probably given milk instead of tea. Moodie hadn't drunk that milk. 'Mother! Don't forget to feed Moodie.'

'Charlotte! As if I would——' At the same moment Mr. Flaxman said, 'Come on, Charlotte! Come on, Adela! The car will catch cold if you don't hurry,' and swept them out of the house.

Meg went slowly upstairs, noticing that the sound of the rain was more insistent in the upper storey of the house. The airing cupboard was in the bathroom. She glanced in quickly and closed the door. She gave the room a rapid tidy, went down, and turned on the wireless.

Meg believed in method. Every morning of the week had its programme; and this was Thursday, when she defrosted the refrigerator, polished the silver and turned out her bedroom—a full morning's work. But today she did none of it, wandering about with a desultory, fidgeting tidiness, taking things up and putting them down again, straightening books on their shelves, nipping dead leaves off the houseplants, while the wireless went on with the Daily Service. There was bound to be a *mauvais quart d'heure*. In fact, everything was well in hand; Charlotte was safely disposed of with the Flaxmans, Moodie was asleep in the airing cupboard and the vet had promised to arrive before midday. It would be quite painless and over in a few minutes. But it was, for all that, a *mauvais quart d'heure*. There are some women, Meg was one of them, in whom conscience is so strongly developed that it leaves little room for anything else. Love is scarcely felt before duty rushes to encase it, anger is impossible because one must always be calm and see both sides, pity evaporates in expedients, even grief is felt as a sort of bruised sense of injury, a resentment that one should have grief forced upon one when one has always acted for the best. Meg's conscience told her that she was acting for the best: Moodie would be spared inevitable suffering, Charlotte protected from a possibly quite serious trauma, Alan undisturbed in his work. Her own distress—and she was fond of poor old Moodie, no other cat could quite replace him because of his associations—was a small price to pay for all these satisfactory arrangements, and she was ready to pay it, sacrificing her own feelings as duty bid, and as common sense also bid. Besides, it would soon be over. The trouble about an active, strongly developed conscience is that it requires to be constantly fed with good works, a routine shovelling of meritorious activities. And when you have done everything for the best, and are waiting about for the vet to come and kill your old cat and can't therefore begin to defrost a refrigerator or turn out a bedroom, a good conscience soon leaves off being a support and becomes a liability, demanding to be supported itself.

The bad quarter of an hour stretched into half an hour, into an hour, into an hour and a quarter, while Meg, stiffening at the noise of every approaching car and fancying with every gust of a fitful rising wind that Moodie was demanding with yowls to be let out of the airing cupboard, tried to read but could not, looked for cobwebs but found none and wondered if for this once she would break her rule of not drinking spirits before lunchtime. She was in the kitchen, devouring lumps of sugar, when the vet arrived. She took him to the bathroom, opened the cupboard door, heard him say, 'Well, old man?'

'Would you like me to stop? Is there anything I can do to help?'

'If you could let me have an old towel.'

She produced the towel, and went to her bedroom where she opened the window and looked out on the rain and the

tossing trees and remembered that everyone must die. A
last she hear the basin tap turned on, the vet washing his
hands, the water running away.

'Mrs. Atwood. Have you got a box?'

'A box?'

He stood in the passage, a tall, red-faced young man, the
picture of health.

'Any sort of carton. To take it away in. A sack would
do.'

She had not remembered that Moodie would require a
coffin. In a flurry of guilt she began to search. There was
a brown paper carrier; but this would not do, Moodie could
not be borne away swinging from the vet's hand. There was
the carton the groceries had come in; but it was too small,
and had Pan Yan Pickles printed on it. At last she found
a plain oblong carton, kept because it was solid and service-
able. Deciding that this would do, she glanced inside and realized that it would not do like that. Moodie could not be
put straight into an empty box: there must be some sort of
lining, of padding. She tore old newspaper into strips and
crumpled the strips to form a mattress; and then, remembering that flowers are given to the dead, she snatched a
couple of dahlias from a vase and scattered the petals on
top of the newspaper. The vet was standing in the bathroom, averting his eyes from the bidet, the towel neatly
folded was balanced on the edge of the basin, and on the
bathroom stool was Moodie's unrecognizably shabby, de
graded, dead body. Before she realized what she was saying,
she had said, 'If you'll hold the box, I'd like to put him in.'

Yet what else could she say? She owed it to Moodie.
She lifted him on her two hands, as she had lifted him so
often. The unsupported head fell horribly to one side, lol-

ling like the clapper of a bell. She got the body in somehow, and the vet closed the lid of the carton and carried it away. She knew she ought to have thanked him, but she could not speak. She had never seen a dead body before—except on food counters, of course.

She went downstairs and drank a stiffish whisky. Her sense of proportion reasserted itself. One cannot expect to be perfect in any first performance. She had not behaved at all as she had meant to when Charlotte was born. It was a pity about the makeshift box; it was a pity not to have thanked the vet; but the essentials had been secured, Charlotte was safe and happy at Hood House, Alan was happy and busy in his laboratory; neither of them need ever know what agony is involved in the process of rationally, mercifully, putting an end to an old pet. She would make a quick lunch of bread and cheese, and then be very busy. She heard a distant peal of thunder, and welcomed the thought of a good rousing thunderstorm. Something elemental would be releasing. After a few more long, grumbling reverberations the storm moved away, but when she went to defrost the refrigerator she found it darkened and cavernous, and the current off throughout the house. The power lines on Ram Down were always getting struck. She left the refrigerator to natural forces, and as she couldn't use the Hoover either, she polished the silver and sat down to do some mending. She was a bad needlewoman; mending kept her mind occupied till a burst of sunlight surprised her by its slant. She had no idea it was so late. Charlotte would be back at any moment.

Just as the current had gone off, leaving the refrigerator darkened and cavernous, the support of a good conscience now withdrew its aid. Charlotte would be back at any moment. Charlotte would have to be told. Time went on. Suppose there had been a car smash? Charlotte mangled and dying at the roadside, and all because she had been got out of the house while the vet was mercifully releasing Moodie? Meg's doing—how could one ever get over such a thing and lead a normal life again?

She was sitting motionless and frantic when Alan came in, switching on the light in the hall.

'Well, Meg—Why are you looking so wrought up? Didn't the vet come? Couldn't he do his stuff?'

'Oh, yes, that was all right. But Charlotte's not back.'

'When did they say they'd bring her?'

'Adela didn't say exactly. She said, a good long day. But it's long over that—Adela knows how particular I am about bedtime.'

'Why not ring up?'

'But I am sure they must have started by now.'

'Well, someone would be about. They've got that cook. What's their number?'

She heard him in the hall, dialling. Then he came back saying the line seemed to be dead. Ten minutes later, a car drew up and Charlotte rushed into the house, followed by Mrs. Flaxman.

'Mother, Mother! It's been so marvellous, it's been so thrilling. We were struck by lightning. There was a huge flash, bright blue, and the telephone shot across the room and broke ever so much china, and there was an awful noise of horses screaming their heads off and Mr. Flaxman tore out to see if the stables had been struck too, and then ran back saying, "They're all right but our bloody roof's on fire." And there were great fids of burning thatch flying about everywhere, and Mr. Flaxman went up a ladder and

I and Mrs. Flaxman got buckets and buckets of water and handed them up to him. And I was ever so useful, Adela said so, wasn't I, Mrs. Flaxman?'

'I don't know what we'd have done without you, my pet,' said Mrs. Flaxman to Charlotte, and to Meg, 'She got very wet, but we've dried her.'

'And then people came rushing up from the village and trod on the bantams.'

'No, nothing's insured except the portraits and the horses. Giles won't, on principle. Yes, calamitous—but it could have been worse. No, no, not at all, it's been a pleasure having her.'

Adela was gone, leaving the impression of someone from a higher sphere in a hurry to return to its empyrean.

For the present, there was nothing to be done but listen to Charlotte and try not to blame the Flaxmans for having let her get so over-excited. Both parents lit cigarettes and prepared themselves for a spell of entering into their child's world; after all, fifteen minutes earlier, they had been fearing for her life. They smoked and smiled and made appropriate interjections. Suddenly her narrative ran out, and she said, 'Where's Moodie?'

For by the time one is ten one knows when one's parents are only pretending to be interested. Back again in a home that had no horses, no bantams, no curly golden armchairs, no portraits of gentlemen in armour and low-necked ladies, was never struck by lightning and gave her no opportunities to be brave and indispensable, Charlotte concentrated on the one faithful satisfaction it afforded and said, 'Where's Moodie?'

Mastering a feeling like stage-fright, Meg said with composure, 'Darling. Moodie's not here.'

'Why isn't he? Has he run away? Has anything happened to him?'

'Not exactly that. But he's dead.'

'Why? Why is he dead? He was quite well this morning. Why is he dead?'

'You know, darling, poor Moodie hasn't really been feeling well for a long time. He was an old cat. He had an illness.'

Charlotte saw Moodie's broad face, and his eyes staring at her with that thirsty expression. Moodie was dead. Mother had explained to her about death, making it seem very ordinary.

'You remember how horrid his breath smelled?'

'Yes. That was his teeth.'

'It wasn't only his teeth. It was something inside that was bound to kill him sooner or later. And he would have suffered a great deal. So the vet came and gave him an injection and put him to sleep. It was all over in a minute.'

Moodie had gone out and sat in the rain. The child's glance moved to the window and remained fixed on the lawn—so green in the sunset that it was almost golden. It was a french window. Without a word, she opened it and went out.

'Poor Charlotte!' said Alan. 'She's taking it very well. I must say, I think you rubbed it in a bit too much. You needn't have said he stank.'

Meg repressed the retort that if Alan could have done it so much better he might perfectly well have done so. In silence, they watched Charlotte walking about in the garden. It was a very small garden, and newly-planted, and the gardens on either side of it were small and newly-planted too, and only marked off by light railings. To Meg, whose childhood had known a garden with overgrown shrubs, laurel hedges, a disused greenhouse and a toad, it seemed an inadequate place to grieve in; but from the 18th century onwards people have turned for comfort to the bosom of nature, and Charlotte was doing so now, among the standard roses and the begonias. She walked up and down, round and round, pausing, walking on again. 'Going round his old haunts,' said Alan. Moodie, as Meg knew, shared her opinion of the garden; he used it to scratch in, but for any serious haunting went to Mopson's Garage where he and the neighbourhood cats clubbed among the derelict cars. A sense of loss pierced her; knowing Moodie's ways had been a kind of illicit Bohemianism in her exemplary, rather lonely life. But it was Charlotte's loss she must think of—and Charlotte's supper, which was long overdue.

'I wish she'd come in—but we mustn't hurry her.'

Alan said, 'She's coming now.'

Charlotte was walking towards the house, walking with a firm tread. Her face was still pale with shock, but her expression was composed, resolved, even excited. I must give her a sedative, thought Meg. Charlotte entered, saying, 'I've chosen the place for his grave.'

After the bungled explanations that one couldn't, that the lawn would never be the same again, that it wasn't their garden, that the lease expressly forbade burying animals had broken down under the child's cross-examination into an admission that there was no body to bury, that the vet had taken it away, that it could not be got back, that it had been disposed of, that in all probability it had been burned to ashes as her parents' bodies would in due course be burned; after Charlotte, declaring she would never forgive them, never, that they were liars and murderers, that she hated them and hoped they would soon be burned to ashes themselves had somehow been got to bed, they sat down, exhausted, not looking at each other.

'That damned cat!'

As though Alan's words had unloosed it, a wailing cry came from overhead.

'O Moodie, Moodie, Moodie!

'O Moodie, Moodie, Moodie!'

Implacable as the iteration of waves breaking on a beach, the wailing cries rang through the house. Twice Meg started to her feet, was told not to be weak-minded, and sat down again. Alan ought to be fed. Something ought to be done. The mere thought of food made her feel sick. Alan was filling his pipe. Staring in front of her, lost in a final imbecility of patience, she found she was looking at the two dahlia stalks whose petals she had torn away.

'O Moodie, Moodie, Moodie!'

The thought of something to be done emerged. 'We must put off that new kitten,' she said.

'Why?'

Completing her husband's exasperation, Meg buried her face in her hands and began to cry.

'O Moodie,' she lamented. 'Oh, my kind cat!'

# A LONG NIGHT

Henry Sparrow had been directed to the endmost of the two-seat tables in the dining car; and as it had grown too dark to look out of the window and dinner was not yet being served and the young man sitting opposite had not struck him as the kind of fellow-traveller he would enjoy talking to he resumed the dissatisfied speculations which the notice above the young man's seat had been intermittently arousing in him during a course of years:

PRIÈRE D'EXIGER UNE NOTE POUR TOUTE
SOMME VERSÉE

The French official mind emerges from an unswervingly applied education, which includes (under grammar) verse forms, the caesura, *rimes riches* and *rimes suffisantes*, together with admired passages of declamation to be scanned, analysed and learned by heart. So it was natural enough that a notice in a *wagon-restaurant* should open as though it meant to be an Alexandrine. But the author couldn't keep it up; he fell into that torrent of syllables and was swept on, helpless, till he clawed himself back onto the classic manner with his '*versée*'—a preposterous word in the circumstances, thought Henry Sparrow, who had learned during the Medium and Advanced French of his school days to associate it with flowers and tears.

The car had filled up, a man had come round with the basket of rolls, the train had entered the Simplon Tunnel and Henry, who did not like being beaten by a trifle, applied himself yet once again to rescuing that foundered Alexandrine. A bold, but permissible, expedient would be to treat the opening as a half line:

*Prière d'exiger*
*Une note, Messieurs les Voyageurs. . . .*

But this only postponed the crisis, besides demanding a larger expanse of public advertising space.

The lights flickered, and went out.

For a moment, no one spoke. The noise of the trains grinding up the incline took over, and was portentous. Someone farther down the car clicked a cigarette lighter; someone else struck a match. A voice from across the table exclaimed, 'Oh, thank God!'

With more clicking of lighters, striking of matches, everyone began to talk. There was a dawn chorus of cheerful expostulations, and car attendants appeared with little lanterns. Under cover of this, Henry said, 'Why? Why "Thank God"?'—for the voice had sounded so abjectly relieved that curiosity was too much for him.

'I always think I've gone blind. Silly, isn't it?'

In the train journey that took Henry to and from his boarding school there had been a certain tunnel—not long enough to warrant lighting up but long enough to impose that darting panic, that interval of accepting the worst. Even when familiarity had taught him not to be an ass he still dreaded the tunnel, because, though it could no longer frighten him, it could remind him how horribly frightened he had been. 'Most people feel like that, at some time or another,' he said. 'Especially when they are young. When one is young, one has a great deal of superfluous fear.

Young animals——' He was about to instance colts when the lights came on again, and the attendants began serving the first course.

There sat the young man whom Henry had decided he would not enjoy talking to. A weedy specimen: long, thin neck, high, spotty forehead, callow chin beard—everything about him was weedy. With his shabby-jaunty air, and his pale eyes flinching in their dark circles of sleeplessness, he was at once pathetic and unprepossessing. But a contact had flashed between them; conversation must be kept up.

'I suppose it was a fuse,' Henry said. 'I'm glad they put it right. The tunnel would seem even more interminable if we had to sit in the dark.'

'How long is it?'

'I believe it takes about twenty minutes.'

'Twenty minutes? I don't call that much. I've been through a tunnel in Norway that takes thirty-eight minutes.'

Henry said 'Really?' and hoped the conversation might now languish.

Presently the young man revived it.

'The whole of this journey strikes me as interminable. I loathe these internationalized trains. They're so artificial. ... *Garçon! Un Coke.*'

'Have you been travelling long?'

'I haven't had a proper sleep for the last four nights. I don't know if you call that long.'

The train had altered its voice. Like an underground stream, it was hurrying down to the valley of the Rhône. Henry, knowing that this was not the solicited inquiry, inquired, 'Have you much farther to go?'

'Liverpool. What's this mess? Veal, I suppose. It's always veal.'

'*A l'Ambassadeur*. In a cream sauce, with mushrooms,' said the attendant, in English.

This is insufferable, thought Henry; I shall get out at Sion. . . . And why not? He had long wanted to hear that venerable organ which had snored and tweedled through so many centuries; he was not particularly expected at home; so why not get out at Sion? All that would be required was the strength of mind to discount the cost of his sleeper and to reclaim his suitcase and passport from the *wagon-lit* attendant. There would be time to finish his veal, which was excellent; then he would assert himself as a freeborn Englishman, rise, pay and escape from the odious young fellow.

Meanwhile the odious young fellow was talking on. 'The only way to travel is on foot. It's the only way you get to know the real country, the real people. Live with peasants and help with the harvest. Drink the local wines. Stay in little fishing ports, go out in the boats, sing, get to know everybody. When I'm in a place like that, I always make a point of going to church.'

'What do you do in Rome?' asked Henry. He knew this would be wasted, and it was.

'Rome? Don't talk to me of Rome. I'd no sooner got into this train than a ghastly slum family was shoved in on top of me—father, mother, three kids, all their earthly belongings in bags and baskets. And they'd come on from Rome—they said so. One of the kids is some sort of cripple, and does nothing but whine and fidget. And his dear Mum does nothing but jump up and down, getting this out of one basket and that out of another, to tempt his appetite. I don't know what they're doing on a rapid. They ought to be in a cattle truck.'

This, too, was overheard by the attendant, who had removed Henry's neat plate and hovered uncertainly over the young man's mauled remains.

'Talking of travelling—yes, take it away, I'm through —I ran into a bit of real life in Turkey. Have you ever been in Turkey?'

'Only on the beaten track.'

'The what? Oh, yes, the beaten track. Well, this wasn't the sort of thing you'd find on the beaten track. It was off in the mountains. I'd been walking all day. I'd seen one shepherd in the morning; after that, no one—just a few eagles. And it had got dark suddenly. You know how suddenly it gets dark in Turkey; even on the beaten track you'd notice that. It looked like a case of under-the-stars for me—not the first time, either—when I saw some tall white things: they were tombstones in a cemetery. And beside it was a broken-down old mosque. Well, I thought, no smoke without fire; where there's dead folks, there's live folks. Sure enough there was a village. Well, knowing how hospitable these mountain Turks are—hospitality's a sacred duty with them—I knocked at a door. No answer. I knocked at another door. No answer. I called. A dog began howling. That was all. There was a storm coming up, and a perishing wind. So I went back to the mosque and curled up just inside. Last thing I knew was the dog howling. When I woke, it was daylight, and the dog was still howling. And the floor of the mosque was covered with stiffs. I must have picked the one place where there wasn't a stiff. And every one of them had spots. Plague spots! Did I hop it? Just think!' said the young man, leaning over the table. 'Just think! If a flea off one of those stiffs had bitten me, I'd have got plague!'

'A near thing,' said Henry. It was the best he could do. The story, told by old Dr. Protheroe, had made a deep impression on him when he was eight years old and newly allowed to sit up for Sunday supper. In the Protheroe version it was typhus, and there was no dog. The dog was a good touch, and if the young man had supplied it, it did him credit. *Ars longa*, thought Henry. Two world wars, the Spanish Influenza epidemic, Auschwitz, Hiroshima had gone by and were in process of being forgotten. Old Dr. Protheroe's story was as lively as ever; in time it would certainly be told on the moon. Art is long, and tough, and never loses a tooth. This Ninon de l'Enclos of a narrative was fastened in the very flesh of the poor braggart sitting below *Prière d'exiger*. By dint of telling, it had become his story, it had happened to him. His neck swelled, his eyes bulged, there was sweat on his forehead; if one had taken his hand, how horribly clammy the palm would be! Now he would dream about it, and cry out in his sleep. But on reflection, the poor wretch would not be in a way for nightmares; he was spending the night in that crowded compartment with the sickly child and the fidgeting mother.

Coffee was served, the case of liqueurs brought round. Henry had a brandy and offered one to the young man.

'No, thanks. I don't drink alcohol. In any form.' Earlier in the conversation, he had been drinking the wine of the country with peasants—but no matter.

Bills were made out and laid on the tables. The head of the service came round with his cashbox. The young man glanced at his bill, pulled out his wallet, put down a couple of notes. The head of the service, a stout, Father-Christmasy Swiss, shook his head. 'These are lire notes, Monsieur. The charge is in francs.'

When the bill had been settled, the young man said to Henry with a limping smile, 'That's done for my breakfast.' It was the first unfeigned remark he had made since his 'Oh, thank God!' and Henry was completely at a loss how to answer it. 'Unless they'll take these.' With a flourish, the young man threw some Turkish notes on the table and looked at Henry as much as to say, 'There! Now do you believe me?'

Henry was prepared to believe the young man had been in Turkey; he had a vivid mind's-eye picture of him going for a walk beyond a bus stop, trembling at every dog, kite and skin eruption. He knew he ought to ask appropriate questions. He also knew that he ought to offer to change the notes. If he had been asked to, he would have done it willingly enough. However, he was glad he had not been asked, as then he would have put himself under an obligation (for every obligation is two-sided, the one who obliges being tied by the acceptance of the one obliged) and he did not want to be under an obligation to this boasting, flinching mongrel, whom he was now quite inordinately disliking. Besides, it was too late. He had thought about it. Such acts are only possible if one does them suddenly, and Henry was not a person who did things suddenly.

A moment later, the suddenness of his action was as surprising as though a rocket had exploded off his lips. He had said, 'You'll go to pieces if you don't get a night's sleep. I'm going to put you in my sleeper.'

'In your sleeper? Very kind of you, I'm sure. But I'm afraid it's out of the question. I'd really rather not.' The refusal, beginning haughtily, ended coyly. It was clear that he had no doubt of Henry's intentions, and that the coyness was a cautious acceptance of them.

'Where's your compartment?' said Henry. 'Two cars down? Good! Then you can pick up your traps on the way. Come on!'

Watching from the corridor, he saw the look of alarm on the mother's face, and the sadness of her gesture as she woke the child who had stretched out into the vacated seat, gathered him to her and settled his feet on a bundle. The young man jerked down a suitcase from the rack, stumbled over the bundle, stumbled against the man who sat in the inner corner nursing a fiddle case and came away, exclaiming, 'My God, what a pigsty!'

'Come on,' said Henry once more. His rage was now sabled with gloom. Not only was he about to put this young cad into his sleeper, he would also have to explain the transfer to the *wagon-lit* attendant. It would probably turn out to be against the regulations. In which case he would . . . He really did not know what he would do, except that nothing on earth should prevent him from doing a thing he would do with the utmost ill-willingness.

The attendant was sitting in his small apartment, looking monkish. He was an immensely tall man, with an inured expression. When he stood up, he did it with a functional agility, as though he were an expanding ladder and part of the equipment. Henry, concentrating on the matter-of-course aspect of thus disposing of a sleeper, almost forgot whom he was proposing to put into it till, with the words, 'This gentleman here', he glanced back at the young man standing behind him. Dirty, hangdog, apprehensive, the young man looked like a criminal hauled before yet another official person who would presently find him out. Inflamed by that chivalry towards oppressed criminals by which a law-abiding Englishman compounds his law-abidingness, Henry prepared to give battle. The attendant shrugged his shoulders and said he must have the gentleman's passport and ticket. The young man produced them with the affable air of one who has again diddled the authorities, and was conducted to the sleeper.

Henry stood in the corridor waiting to tip. The attendant reappeared. 'I'm afraid I can't offer Monsieur another sleeper,' he said. 'And the train is very full tonight. However, some people may be getting out at Lausanne. You might find a seat then. It is possible.' His voice had a skin of solicitude over a granite disapprobation. Scratch a Frenchman and you'll find a schoolmistress, thought Henry, quite unfairly. Deciding that he would go back to the restaurant car for another brandy, he began to walk through the train. In the corridor of a first-class a man had pulled down a window and was leaning out. He was so absorbed that he made no attempt to move out of the way, so Henry paused and looked out, too. The train slowed down; then, with the eccentricity of night expresses, it came massively to a halt. The black mountain silhouette remained fixedly against the sky, the improbable sparkles of light on its flanks settled into a social pattern. He could hear the noise of a waterfall. If he had got out at Sion he would have spared himself all this shame of false kindness and futile rage—besides having a bed to look forward to. The train began to move, a woman's voice said, 'For God's sake, Winthrop,' the man went into his compartment. Henry walked on. Almost unawares, he recognized the compartment the young man had quitted.

There they were, the man nursing the fiddle case, the

stout man sitting opposite, the family beyond. The two little girls had fallen asleep, clasped together and moving as one body with the sway of the train. Beyond them, the father drowsed. The boy seemed to be asleep, too; at any rate his eyes were shut in his pained, twitching face. Only the mother sat erect and wakeful, supporting the boy's head on her lap. Her face was hidden by the folds of the dull black kerchief tied under her chin, but Henry knew by her attitude that she had composed herself to wakefulness as others compose themselves to sleep. Just as her sad gesture had moved him before, her attitude moved him now. She was small, thin, meanly built; but she was one of those beings whose movements and postures have the infallible aristocracy of a long lineage of labour, hardship and duty. She could no more go wrong with a gesture, he thought, than she could go wrong paring a potato. The boy stirred. She turned her head to look down at him. Her glance went on to the two little girls, to the packages in the rack, to Henry looking in. She leaned forward, careful not to disturb the boy, and touched her husband's knee. Instantly, he came out of his drowse. She said something, and glanced again to the door, and extended her hand palm uppermost over the space between the boy and the stout man in the corner. Henry shook his head, but at the same moment the husband spoke to the stout man, who pulled open the door, saying, 'The Signora says that if you are looking for a seat, there is one here.'

'It is most kind of the Signora,' said Henry. 'But I could not think of disturbing her. I shall certainly find a seat farther on.'

'For that matter,' said the man with the fiddle case, 'if you don't mind waiting a little longer, I shall be getting out at Lausanne, and you can have my seat without disturbing anybody.'

They all did her bidding, as though she were a queen.

Just before Lausanne, the man with the fiddle case came into the corridor, touched Henry's shoulder and said, 'You can go in now.' He obeyed, and sat down beside the two little girls. The woman looked across at him. Her grave, unsmiling face was momentarily expressive of a grave satisfaction; then she looked away and the black drapery hooded her again.

No one spoke. From time to time the boy twitched and moaned. The stout man snored quietly. Then the elder of the little girls, who had woken up, said with a look of delight, 'He's like the sea!'

The mother's finger went up to her lips, but the stout man snored on, and presently the father said to Henry, 'It is natural. Our home is by the sea. Besides, I am a fisherman.'

'A hard life,' said Henry.

'Yes, you are right; a hard life, and a poor livelihood. But it has compensations. One can pick up driftwood on the beach. Sometimes we even find coal. But it does not burn well; the sea has got into it.'

'Once I picked up a toothbrush,' said the little girl.

She was easier to understand than her father, who turned to her when he was at a loss for the Italian for some dialect word. Clasping her sister and swaying in unison with her, she interpreted, and helped on the conversation with comments of her own. They were Sardinians; none of them except the father had been off the island till now, when they were all going to London in England—except Rocco and the hens. Rocco had been coming too but Uncle

Dante said that the English customs officers would put him in a prison called the Quarantina; though he had never bitten anybody and had very few fleas.

'The boy's dog, you understand,' said the father. 'A pet. It is because of my poor boy that we are going to London. There is a hospital in London that can cure such children, so my wife's brother says. He and his family live in London. He keeps a tavern——'

'A restaurant,' corrected the little girl.

'—a restaurant, and students from that hospital go there, and he spoke to one of them about our Gianpaolo. And in the end, suddenly, we heard that all was arranged—the doctor, the bed in the hospital, our permits, our journey. Dante is paying for it all. There is even to be a cabin on the boat. A cabin!' He shook with laughter at the joke of a fisherman going to sea in a cabin.

'Your brother-in-law is a good friend.'

'Oh, yes, Dante is good, very good. And he is rich. He has done very well; he makes a great deal of money.'

The mother, who till now had been silent, looked full at Henry. 'You too are good,' she said in a stern voice. 'You gave up your place in the train to that young man. I saw what was happening. I understood.'

He lowered his eyes. He did not know how to answer. If he was silent, he would appear to concur. He certainly could not enter into the truth; and the usual 'Not at all, it was nothing' would not serve, since there had been an implied reception in her words so that to belittle his merit would be to slight her approval. He was deciding, rather romantically, that the only offering he could make to this remarkable woman would be to leave her her illusion when, raising his eyes, he saw that no answer was called for.

Having paid him his due, she had dismissed him from her mind and was offering the child a biscuit.

He wished he could dismiss himself from his own mind. He had felt a glow of pleasure when the stern voice addressed him. The discovery that he had been noticed, pondered on—that he had become a person to her, been received—would have been delightful, if it had not depended on that mistaken word 'good'. After the malice with which he had listened to the young man, and probably envy, too, since he would not have felt such animated dislike for someone nearer his own age; after that arrogant wealthy man's offer of the sleeper, made on an impulse that couldn't have had a spark of kindness in it (since when it was read as an improper advance he was merely glad of another reason for disliking); after the inertia of not getting out at Sion and so retreating with some remnants of self-respect, it was not easy to submit to an imputation of goodness. Yet by degrees it became easier. Her mistake was in no way his doing; it was not even the total condemnation his middle-class conscience felt it to be—a conscience rating goodness at rarity value and shaped from nursery onwards by such estimating phrases as 'good as gold'. These people had a different, perhaps unworldly, outlook on goodness, and apparently did not find it more surprising than, say, rain. A torrential rain comes to be acknowledged as the flood of such or such a year; a torrential goodness comes to be acknowledged as a saint; but apart from extremes, goodness and rain are something naturally to be expected. So the father had agreed that Dante was good, very good; but it was Dante's enabling riches he dwelt on, the riches that were conveying the family to London and Gianpaolo to the hospital. Such an outlook, at once practical and discerning, was very probably quite a common one—at any rate among people who seldom hear the term 'philanthropy' and do not daily receive printed appeals on behalf of the blind, the starving, the homeless, the underprivileged, the unconverted to this religion or that. Very likely the stout man sitting opposite also enjoyed this outlook—which was why he was able to snore so peacefully. The little girl was quite right: he snored like the sea.

The train rushed on through the darkness, and in the darkness waves fell on the beach, broke against the cliffs, and the sea closed and relaxed its embrace of the island. A traveller by air would look down and say, 'I suppose that's Sardinia.' Which way (for one was free to decide) should the plane be travelling—east or west? Henry was nosing his way into sleep when the flash and roar of a train running counter to theirs recalled him to where he was, and why. He realized that it might be possible for him to redeem his imputed goodness. His riches enabled him to command porters.

'I hope there will be someone meeting you at Victoria,' he said to the father.

'Victoria? I don't know about Victoria. Dante will know. He is meeting us at the port of Calais.'

The mother nodded, her face glittering with excitement as though it were a rock dashed with a sudden spray. If Dante resembled his sister, thought Henry, their meeting would be a sight worth seeing. Dante, indeed, was the answer to everything. By asking the address of Dante's restaurant it would be possible to see these people again; perhaps, at last, be of some use to them; at any rate, see them. Meanwhile, he had entered the restaurant, where Dante was walking about with a peacock under his arm, feeding it with grapes. Coming up to Henry's table he said, 'Have you brought my sister's hat? If she is going to be Queen of Scotland, she will need several hats.' Looking at the peacock, Henry remarked, 'I suppose that is the Papal Blessing.' Even in his dream, he felt pleased with this perspicacity: not every Englishman would have known it. So, in a light slumber, he went lightly from one dream to another, conscious in another region of his mind that the dreams were gay and harmless and that he would come to no harm among them. From time to time, he woke more completely and saw the wakeful mother, sitting composedly, her hooded head erect and sleek like a bird's. Not since his childhood, when the wind blew in the chimney and the black cat lay under the scarlet eiderdown, had he slept so confidently.

Somewhere in the middle of this strange night without time or locality, he was nudged awake to share in a meal of bread and stony-hard sausage and rough sweet wine. The stout man had been awakened, too. He was a motor salesman. Hearing Henry's English accent, he told how his cousin, a prisoner in England and working for a farmer, had slashed his leg with a bill-hook, and how the farmer's wife, leaving all else, had driven him to the doctor for an anti-tetanus injection. If there was so much science and good will even in a rough country place, there was no saying what a London doctor would not be able to do for the little boy—and should this fail, there was Lourdes.

At the mention of Lourdes, the father's face hardened. Seeing that he had said the wrong thing, the motor salesman offered peppermints all round and then produced a very clean handkerchief which he knotted into a conjurer's rabbit. The rabbit frisked about among the children, tickling them with its ears and pulling peppermints and coins out of pockets and hair ribbons. 'Look out, look out! He'll be after your biscuit. Oho, what he has found now?' A coin fell on the floor. The little girls made a dive for it. The boy, escaping from his mother's hold, leaned down, lost his balance and fell. Screaming with pain and terror he lay writhing among their feet. When his father tried to lift him up he squirmed away, hideously agile, hauling himself along on his elbows with his useless legs trailing after him, striking his head against whoever's hand came near him.

'Fool!' said Henry to the motor salesman.

The motor salesman's horrified, crimsoned face did not alter; probably he had not heard, because of the noise the child was making. No one else uttered a word of blame. The mother knelt down beside the child; she made no attempt to touch him but kept up a wordless noise of condolence. Half grunt, half creak, it was more like a tree's voice than a woman's. The boy turned his head and spat at her. Instantly, she had her arms round him and in the same flow of movement had lifted him back onto the seat. 'Brute! Brutes!' he said between sobs.

'*Ciao!*' The father spoke under his breath, with a life-time of accepted endurance in his voice.

Presently, like reflections in a shaken pond, they settled again, were the same family travelling to London with a sick child, the same pair of well-meaning outsiders. The mother's kerchief, loosened in the struggle, had fallen back. Tears of fatigue ran down her unshielded face. Sleep was mastering her, harsh as death in its oncoming. Twice she reeled forward, twice she jerked herself awake and erect again. Henry got up, saying to the motor salesman that they should move to the corridor. The father misunderstood, and began to apologize for the disturbance.

'The Signora must lie down. She is worn out. You must take the boy from her,' said Henry; and to his amazement he found himself lifting the sleeping child and planting him on the father's lap. As the child's weight was taken away, she put out a groping hand. The elder little girl took hold of it, patted it, and laid it gently back on her breast. She was dead asleep before they had settled her at full length, with a bundle under her head and her feet decently covered with a shawl. Even then, the father made a last attempt at hospitality, pointing out that the two little girls took up no more room than one person, so that with the boy held on his knee there would still be places for the two gentlemen.

Constrained together by what they had been through, Henry and the motor salesman stood in the corridor, keeping up a desultory conversation. Dijon had been left behind; the muteness of the first light was like a reproach to human activities. 'Why go further?' it seemed to say. 'Why all these purposes?' The motor salesman remarked that it would have been better to try Lourdes before London; whatever a person's opinions might be, there was no harm in showing a little civility; and there was no reason to think that the child of Communist parents would not stand as good a chance as any other—even a better chance, as it would be a more beautiful miracle. Henry felt the familiar squirming of inquiry always aroused in him by religious remarks but he had learned from experience that only Dissenters like to have their religious remarks followed up. He praised the behaviour of the two little girls. The motor salesman agreed. Presently they parted.

I shall never see her again, Henry thought, for I can't go back now and ask the name of Dante's restaurant. They would not think it odd. But I should. For a quiet man who minded his own business, he had performed a sufficiency of odd acts during the course of this long night. Since entering Switzerland, he had thrust a young man into his sleeper because he loathed him, prepared himself to fight a *wagon-lit* attendant, compelled a motor salesman out of his corner seat, and fallen in love with a fisherman's wife—who had addressed exactly one remark to him, and that on a false assumption. He had fallen in love with her, and almost immediately had fallen asleep in her presence—as contentedly, as reposefully, as though the physical act of love had taken place between them. A long night!—unquestioned, violent and inconsequential as a dream. Even now, the sun had not risen, and the mists were sleeping in the woodlands, and the odious young man was sleeping in his sleeper.

As he watched, the sky opened like a wound and a glaring tinsel streaked the horizon. Before midday, they would be safe in Dante's keeping. It was too ambitious, it was almost blasphemous, to hope that their breakfast would have escaped Dante's consideration; for all that, he would ask about it after leaving Paris, where the breakfast car came on. The brief glare of sunrising waned and went out; daylight showed a low ceiling of cloud. In Paris it would be raining.

In Paris it was raining. Yellow mackintoshes, white mackintoshes, black mackintoshes emerged from suburban trains and disappeared like a flitting of butterflies. Long dead, and grown quite respectable and undebatable, the French Impressionists continue to paint Paris. The canvases of the Gare du Nord replaced the canvases of the Gare de Lyon. Presently the hand bell would be rung down the corridor. Though he was rumpled and unshaven, he would have breakfast before he faced the odious young man, the disapproving attendant.

The noise of the hand bell approached, its associations so compelling that the smell of coffee seemed to be approaching with it. On the heels of the ringer came a man carrying a breakfast tray. The clatter of crockery ceased, a door was opened, there was an acclaim of voices. The little girls led it, but everyone was talking, and they all sounded happy and unconstrained—as they would be, of course, now that his formalizing presence was removed. So Henry went and ate his solitary breakfast, and prolonged the solitude as long as his self-respect would allow him to. When he came to walk past the compartment that was Sardinia, he allowed himself to glance in. The mother was replaiting the younger daughter's hair, the father was rolling a cigarette. No one saw him. There seemed to be a great deal more hand baggage than during the night, but that was because much of it had been taken down from the rack and opened to get things out. When an adventure is over, it is over. Only the adventure's grudging begetter remained—the young man but for whose inability to recognize a peasant family when he met it Henry would not have entered the Sardinian compartment. No doubt he also had been unpacking and expanding. If he starts being grateful to me, thought Henry; if he has the effrontery to utter a word of thanks ... However, this did not seem very likely.

The *wagon-lit* attendant was in his cell, bundling sheets into a laundry sack. 'Your sleeper's ready for you,' he said. 'I expect you'll be glad to be back in it, and to have it to yourself.' Having watched the first arrow quiver in the outer ring, he aimed the second at the bull's-eye. 'Your friend has left the train, you know. He collected his passport and his ticket to London, and got out at the Gare de Lyon.' Barely glancing at the effect of his words, he showed Henry into his tidied, passionless sleeper and left him to think it over. Postponing emotion, Henry shaved.

Shaving was a thing that Henry did very well, but shave as he might, he was not able to dispel his bristling uneasiness. The event was so exactly what he would have wished that he could not feel satisfied with it. There must be a catch in it somewhere. The young man would reappear, having got out to buy a paper, or hoping to change his Turkish notes. But if so, why did he take his suitcase with him? Suppose he had killed himself in a lavatory?—with a revolver taken from the suitcase? This disposed of the suitcase but not of the young man. His body would be found, the attendant would testify that Henry had put him in the sleeper, a guilty association would be manifest to all, and by the time Henry had extricated himself from the processes of French law, dozens of starving relations would have sprung up in Liverpool. There would be a widowed mother—he was the kind of young man who has 'Widowed Mother' stamped on his brow. Henry had noticed it, along with the pimples, beneath *Prière d'exiger* when the lights came on again in the dining car. *'Priere d'exiger'* . . . ominous words. It was going to be one of those transactions you don't get out of till the uttermost farthing has been accounted for. All ill-considered kind actions end calamitously—at any rate, most of Henry's did. One should learn to leave kind actions to the young, who are not endangered by them since they rarely perform them.

Calmed by these general reflections, Henry began to think on broader lines. He thought he would go to sleep. He settled himself, and closed his eyes. They hadn't closed comfortably. He opened them again and saw that the sleeper wasn't quite what it had been. Something was missing. What was missing was the slow wag of his overcoat on its hanger. So that was it! The odious young man had left the train because it was a safe and simple way of stealing a good overcoat. Warm in a good overcoat, he would wait till the next train, and then continue his journey. Henry heaved a sigh of relief. His mind was at rest. He need never give another thought to that odious young man, and when he got to London he would buy a new overcoat.

There was a knock; the door opened. The attendant came in, and he held the overcoat. He had observed, he said with specious tact, that Monsieur's friend had dropped cigarette ash on it. To avert any further mishap, he had taken it away.

The coat was put on the hanger, and resumed its faintly mesmerizing wag. It was a good coat, and Henry was attached to it; under different circumstances he would have been glad to see it again. But now it came as a monitor, and told him he was not done with that young man after all. He would not reappear, he would not be found dead in a lavatory—these silly fancies had gathered up their improbably trailing skirts and fled like ghosts at sunrise. What remained was the real young man, who had left the train with his shabby suitcase, and no good solid overcoat, and no apparent reason. There he stood on the platform, hunching his narrow shoulders against the wet, wolfish cold. No overcoat, no breakfast, no reason. No real reason. No possible reason at all that Henry could see, except a reason which irresistibly imposed itself on his mind, forcing him to admit its validity, its tit-for-tat symmetrically. For if the odious young man had felt a reciprocal dislike, and had nursed it all night, tossing in luxury on a bed he had been forced into, and in the morning had realized that he would be expected to put up some show of thanks to the odious old fellow who at any moment would reappear with his chilblained civility, he might very well have had the courage of his animosity and got out in Paris—as Henry had failed to do at Sion.

Printed in Great Britain
by Amazon

15043571R00128